KU-072-828

Rich Hall is famed for his brilliant stand-up routines and comic creation Otis Lee Crenshaw. He appears regularly on TV including several of his own TV series. He won two Emmys for his work with David Letterman.

BOLTON LIBRARIES

BT 178 5282 X

Also by this author

SNIGLETS
SELF HELP FOR THE BLEAK
THINGS SNOWBALL
I BLAME SOCIETY

magnificent
bastards

rich hall

ABACUS

First published in Great Britain in 2009 by Abacus
This paperback edition published in 2010 by Abacus

Copyright © 2009 Rich Hall

The moral right of the author has been asserted.

*All characters and events in this publication, other than
those clearly in the public domain, are fictitious
and any resemblance to real persons,
living or dead, is purely coincidental.*

All rights reserved.
No part of this publication may be reproduced, stored in a retrieval system, or
transmitted, in any form or by any means, without the prior permission in writing
of the publisher, nor be otherwise circulated in any form of binding or cover other
than that in which it is published and without a similar condition including this
condition being imposed on the subsequent purchaser.

A CIP catalogue record for this book
is available from the British Library.

ISBN 978-0-349-12133-8

Typeset in Times New Roman by Palimpsest Book Production Limited,
Falkirk, Stirlingshire
Printed and bound in Great Britain by Clays Ltd, St Ives plc

Papers used by Abacus are natural, renewable and recyclable
products sourced from well-managed forests and certified
in accordance with the rules of the Forest Stewardship Council.

Mixed Sources
Product group from well-managed
forests and other controlled sources
www.fsc.org Cert no. SGS-COC-004081
© 1996 Forest Stewardship Council

Abacus
An imprint of
Little, Brown Book Group
100 Victoria Embankment
London EC4Y 0DY

An Hachette UK Company
www.hachette.co.uk

www.littlebrown.co.uk

To Syd and Pat

BOLTON LIBRARIES	
1785282X	
Bertrams	24/11/2010
	£7.99
HO	

contents

fifty-cent words

OUR FAMILY WAS constantly moving. My dad was a marginally employed salesman whose miserable finances seemed to be slowly turning my mom into a husk of a human. I, on the other hand, adored him for this one clear fault: his wildly misguided embrace of success.

Most of our lives up to that point had been spent in trailer parks and housing projects. This time, however, we'd found a *real* house. It was on Brandywine Avenue, a relocation meant to be viewed by my mom as an ascent in status, though it was just a two-bedroom dormer that my dad described as nothing more than 'a piss and a look around'. The yard was full of car batteries and old tyres. You could smell the place from a hundred yards away because a big sheltering magnolia had gotten its roots into the septic tank and gone berserk. My dad never bothered to do anything about it. This inattention to larger-than-life disasters was probably the reason my mom would

1

eventually leave. He was a ferocious drinker, my dad, who squandered entire afternoons sprawled on the porch playing Roger Miller records and getting tanked. When the beer ran out, he would walk down to the tavern at the bottom of the street and sell an insurance policy to a drunk.

He taught me, at a young age, the value of oration.

'Once you've got the drop on public speaking, you've got the whole thing licked,' he would say. 'The secret is to make people think they're *helping you*.'

Some days he would take me with him to the tavern. He would perch himself on a bar stool, tantalising his beer to make it last, dipping his tongue into the foam head, re-examining it, then forcing a long draw down his throat. No one ever made a beer look more delicious. Fortified, he would set about haranguing cranks and drifters – not much different from him – on the possibilities of comprehensive health coverage. He was fearless at this, with a special knack for sussing out military vets. He had a US Navy anchor tattooed on one forearm and a US Army eagle on the other. From what I'd gathered, my dad had never even been *near* a military base.

'You was a swabbie? So was I!' he would say to some unsuspecting mark, then roll up a sleeve to reveal the appropriate tattoo. He would shuffle me off with a dime for the pinball machine, and I would stand there and work the plungers, listening to his spiel.

'USS *Iowa*. I went from bosun's mate to chief petty officer in record time, look it up you don't believe me.' (As if such achievements were public record.) 'What are you drinking? *Hey, bartender, this navy man's glass is leaking!* Yessiree, the old *Iowa*. Those were the days. Did you know, did you know, *did you know* we had an

2

eight-hundred-seat movie theatre aboard that thing? We'd send a fireball up the ass of one of those religious kamikazes and be watching *Hell in the Pacific* before they'd even hit the water. Now let me ask you this, mate. For all our efforts, for all we did to preserve the name of freedom . . . do you think the Veterans Administration gives two shits about us? Oh sure, they'll promise us anything, 'cos they don't want scenes in their waiting rooms. But once behind the curtain, pal, they're red-pencilling everything. You're goddamn lucky to get an aspirin. And then they come in like goddamn preachers, hat in hand, and tell you they've done all they can humanly do, and your ass is out on the pavement like that, I mean *just that fast*. And this is the consideration you receive for serving your goddamn country? Now just give me one goddamn minute of your time: *tell me about your family.*'

It didn't matter what was described: twelve kids or two goldfish and a boa constrictor. My dad's response was automatic and forthright.

'Obviously they mean everything to you. Now I *need* your confidence.'

He would pull a brochure from his inside coat pocket and spread it across the counter, gesturing over the words as if they were salvation, a lifeboat in a sea of Formica.

'I cannot go into it at this time, but let me say only this: you have heard of the single mustard seed, which, when planted, grows into a sheltering canopy? Well that is what this policy brings to you and your loved ones. A canopy of comprehensive health care that will extend far beyond your own years. *And* . . .' here he leaned in for emphasis, 'there is a special application of these wonders that applies *only* to veterans such as yourself. Here, read it yourself. *Bartender, two more!*'

The policies, underwritten by a post office box in

3

Lowell, Massachusetts, only cost twenty-five dollars. But my dad, in his inebriated moments, possessed a genius for convincing vets they'd been turned out by their government like old pack mules. He aimed to save them. And each policy that he sold saved *him*, or at the very least reconstituted him like frozen orange juice.

That June, when I turned twelve, he presented me with a book.

'This,' he intoned, 'is *Roget's Thesaurus*.' He savoured the exquisite pronunciation of the volume's title. 'In it, you will learn the words that will be the key to all future success.'

'Thanks,' I replied lamely. I was expecting baseball stuff.

I spent that summer memorising words. Unfortunately it made it impossible for me to speak directly on any subject.

Our shabby new neighbourhood sat on the cusp of Myers Park, the *affluent* part of Charlotte. There was no gilded gradation of wealth to announce this. You just walked to the top of Brandywine and it suddenly gave way to a boulevard of stately oaks and mock-Tudor castles. There were boutiques that sold pecan specialities or things made entirely from pine cones, places that took great titular licence to announce themselves 'shoppes' not shops. The dental clinic called itself Teeth, Ltd.

There was a country club here with a handsome swimming pool. I'd made friends with another kid from my street, Herschel Stikeleather, whose stoat-like features and dimwittedness appealed to me because they made me feel instantly superior. Every day that summer, Herschel and I sneaked into the country club, *walked* in, actually: none

4

of the staff seemed to even notice. The pool was a respite from the withering Carolina humidity. The loudspeakers would have been playing something redolently summery and southern: the Bar-Kays, the Lovin' Spoonful, Hugh Masekela, the air a dazzling *array, aggregation, assortment* of chlorine and Coppertone.

In those frictionless days any drama was mentionable and gauged as either a spectacular achievement or a mortifying failure. Thus on an otherwise uneventful afternoon in August, Herschel called me over to one side of the pool. He was floating at water's edge, trying to unravel a mystery. The country club had put up a new hand-painted sign:

WELCOME TO OUR OOL. PLEASE SWIM CAREFULLY
PS YOU'LL NOTICE THERE'S NO 'P' IN OUR 'OOL'

Herschel couldn't seem to make sense of this. To him, the owners had made a mistake spelling 'pool' and then, for some inexplicable reason, *acknowledged* their mistake.

'If they misspelled the word,' he reasoned, 'how come they didn't just tear it up and start over again?' His belief in the infallibility of adults seemed shaken.

'It's a joke,' I said. 'They don't want you peeing in the pool.'

I thought I was pretty clear with that explanation, but Herschel just kept staring at the sign.

'That ain't how you spell "pee",' he concluded.

I decided Herschel's stupidity was a chronic state and all attempts to cure it would probably end up creating their own set of problems. I turned my attention to Elise Alderman, with whom I'd become infatuated and who was, that very moment, at the opposite end of the pool, splayed along the blue-tiled edge, one tanned leg idly swirling about in the water.

Elise had fantastic blue eyes so alluring they cancelled any other detriments, namely her teeth, which were encased in some kind of insane orthodontic structure that resembled scaffolding. She'd stared at me only ever once, early in the summer, but that was all the incitement I needed to be swept along by something thrilling that I had no interest in understanding. Elise's advanced age – thirteen, I figured – seemed to me to make her self-possessed, exotic even. I was convinced her affections were attainable if I could merely demonstrate a degree of sophistication beyond my twelve years. This I intended to achieve by impressing her with my vocabulary.

I swam toward her like someone drifting lazily down the Niagara River unaware the Big Fall was just around the bend. I ducked underwater then surfaced beside her like an otter.

'Hi,' I said.

'Hi,' she said.

After that I didn't say anything else for too long a time. It would have been hard for her not to notice the nervous energy exuding forth from me, but the silence went on for so long that there was a danger of me actually appearing retarded. None of my thesaurus words were yet coming to mind.

Then, from the other end of the pool, Herschel Stikeleather hit the water with a thundercrack: a disastrous high dive, eliciting paroxysms of hooting and catcalls. We watched as he emerged from the pool sheepishly.

'That was just asinine,' said Elise, thankfully cutting the ice. *Asinine*. Her choice of word was so astounding, I decided maybe I should cut any notions of small talk and begin discussing our warm mutual future together.

'Have you been staring at me?' she suddenly asked me.

'I find you *alluring*,' I replied.

'Find me what?'

'*Ardourous,*' I said, not entirely convinced that was a word.

Elise Alderman made a kind of figure-eight movement with her head. She seemed to be either evaluating me or signalling to someone, I wasn't sure.

'I have a boyfriend, Trip Ware,' she said.

As if cued, an older boy approached us. He was lanky and well muscled, sporting a pair of baggies: gaudy over-sized trunks favoured by professional surfers. I figured him for an eighth- or ninth-grader, an age gap that might as well be measured in decades.

He stood over us, silhouetted in a *High Noon* stance.

'What are you saying to my girlfriend?' Trip asked flatly. Ridiculously, I answered:

'I was *acquainting* myself.'

Trip stepped forward to the edge of the pool. He was dangling a Coke bottle delicately by the neck, a sartorial effect that only enhanced the underlying threat of danger.

'*Awhat?*'

'Acquainting . . .' I repeated, then just kind of tapered off, realising words were not going to save me and that probably I'd thrown away a good part of my summer staring at them.

'Get out of the pool,' he instructed.

I believe I understood right then what people mean when they talk about time standing still. I was aware everyone was watching us, hoping for another humiliating disaster to highlight their afternoon. Underwater, I involuntarily let fly and began wailing away on Elise's leg, my first inkling of irony and its many wonderful utilities.

7

'Get out,' he said again.

I climbed out with a sickening sense of doom, searching desperately for some offhanded ambiguity that might distract him from physically assaulting me.

'Tell me, Trip,' I said. 'Where can I *acquire* a pair of these baggies you're wearing?'

'They don't come in kids' sizes,' he smirked.

'I'm not a kid. How much do they cost?'

Trip lifted the Coke bottle, stared at it consideredly, then said: 'More than your dad makes in a year.' He blew across the rim of the bottle and made a perfect freight-train sound.

Then he punched me. I could hear the sound of his fist popping against the bone in my face, and then I was in the water.

'That's enough!' Elise Alderman cried. Trip stood there waiting for me to come out of the water.

Finally he turned and spoke to the onlookers.

'Ya'll go on,' he said.

They hesitated in their disappointment.

'Go on. The show is over.'

Elise stood up to follow him, turned toward me for just an instant and made what I thought was an extraordinary concession.

'They're twenty-five dollars,' she said. 'You can get them at Tate-Browns.'

For a long time I just trod water in the pool. *More than your dad makes in a year.* That someone would use their fists to make such economic distinctions was a real eye-opener.

That afternoon I went home and dressed in my best clothes, meaning to look earnest. I walked through the dilapidated part of town until I reached an area of flourishing

8

subdivisions where the red clay and Norfolk pines had been violently upended to accommodate row after row of new homes. The developers had named these enclaves with some distorted vision of European Romanticism. Breton Acres. The Cotswolds. Stonehenge. Valhalla. Napoleon's Retreat. The Bridge at Remagen. Europe's glorious past raped and repackaged behind a colonial brick entrance gate with a water feature and a banner screaming *Move in Today!* Still, these neighbourhoods seemed to emanate newness and vigour: ideal sales territory. I had one of my dad's policy brochures in my hand and a sort of absurd notion of simply strutting up to a door, announcing myself and making a sales pitch so outlandish that the homeowner would be humoured into buying insurance.

What was behind this? The sting of Trip's words, his implication that beyond the summer's revelry lay a more serious world: the world of privilege. I wanted money.

I stood in the middle of the street, surveying the homes. The lawns were yet to give up any grass, and the asphalt under my feet felt new and soft, like an oatmeal cookie. Summer dark was just starting to loom and each house now seemed foreboding. I imagined angry red-faced owners slamming doors in my face.

Eventually I just walked up to a porch and pushed a doorbell. A young man answered the door. His hair was wet and brushed back, maybe from having just showered, and he wore a baggy Duke University sweatshirt that made him seem instantly affable and uncomplicated.

'Good evening. My name is Richard Hall,' I said, offering a firm handshake. Hand gestures, I'd remembered, were supposed to fend off objections.

'Hello, Richard Hall.' He shook my hand.

'Thank you.'

'What can I do for you?'

'I'm working my way into Duke University.'

'I see. That's very ambitious.'

'Thank you. But I need your help.'

'If you're selling magazines, we've already—'

'Oh no, no, no, no. I'm selling something far more important than magazines. You have heard of the mustard seed that grows into a uh . . . big . . .'

'You selling seeds?'

'Tell me about your family.'

The about-face of this question was mercifully interrupted by the appearance of the man's wife, who came up and peered over his shoulder.

'What is it?' she said.

'Fella says he wants to go to Duke,' the man said.

'Wonderful,' said his wife.

In the end, they invited me in. We sat at the dining table, and every time I waffled in my sales pitch they simply gave me a bit of steady encouragement, like directors talking a nervous actor through a part. I rollicked through my arsenal of remembered words. Is your current policy *adequate*? In the event of *adversity* are you *amply* covered? I told them they were an *astonishingly* lucky couple.

'How's that?'

'I am *authorised* to sell you this complete insurance package for twenty-five dollars!'

They both feigned shock.

'My God, we're stretched pretty thin these days what with this new house and all,' said the husband, reaching for his wallet. He extracted a pair of dollar bills. 'But here's a coupla bucks toward that scholarship.' Before I could even thank them they were ushering me out the door. I concluded the transaction by effusively waving at them from the yard like some kind of clodhopper. I was elated. It occurred to me right there that all I really needed to sell was a charm routine.

Throughout the evening, I made heady refinements to my sales technique, scrutinising each house carefully for exploitable clues. If the car in the driveway had a university decal, that became the school I was working my way through. Religious insignias on the door made me an aspiring divinity student.

No one purchased a policy, but that, of course, wasn't the point. I was rewarded purely on presentation: a dollar here, two there, sometimes five. By the end of the evening I had easily amassed twenty-five dollars and the following afternoon arrived at the pool in a billowing pair of ghastly Birdwell brand surf baggies that announced me like a tall mast on a very puny boat.

Trip Ware got the message right away. He understood I was mocking him and decked me again.

In the autumn I enrolled at Myers Park Junior High. Almost immediately, I was made aware of the specific dress style among the boys: *prep*, to which they adhered with almost fetishistic allegiance. Skirmishes were constantly breaking out, usually evolved from a fashion slur of some kind. French cuffs, for example, were 'gay'. Weejun loafers should not be defiled by inserting a penny in the slots, etc. Thumbed copies of the latest *Gentlemen's Quarterly* passed under desks like porn. This was a world of thirteen-year-old fops whose leader, Trip Ware – gridiron star and all-around reigning pug – presided with complete entitlement. His Oxford cotton shirts were starched to within an inch of their lives, his khaki trousers knife-creased, his monogrammed slip buckle belt lustrous. He seemed incapable of losing face, while I stayed confined to the margins, the humiliation of the

11

country club beatings hanging on me like a sandwich board.

Hershel and I attended school football games together, sitting on exposed rickety bleachers high up and away from the other students. October was in the air, the trees shabby with half-shed leaves. We watched with detached amusement as the football team allowed its opponent to run up the half-time score to 77–0. The players refused to tackle anyone lest they soil their uniforms. From the bench, the coach pleaded with them for his own dignity.

'I have to show my face in this town,' he brayed, near tears. 'Could you please just *try* to look like you're upset when the other team scores?'

Trip Ware played halfback. There was something about his haughty gait, his seeming disconnection from the debacle of the game itself that was more attractive to the crowd than watching the rest of the team get pummelled mercilessly. When he *did* get tackled, the crowd bleated its sympathy. He would pick himself up off the ground, and in those moments I was beside myself with joy. Still, it wasn't the courage I was looking for.

I ended up sharing an elective class, civics, with him. He took a prominent place near the back of the classroom. The other kids lingered around him before the bell and during class give him plenty of space in which to push his desk back against the wall, lace his fingers behind his head and possess the room. I sat a few rows ahead and felt him staring black X-rays into the back of my neck.

Our instructor, Miss Mackie, was a thuggish woman of astounding *amplitude*. One afternoon in November she was attempting to explain How The Post Office Works to a decidedly uninterested class. She'd brought along various postage stamps for illustrative effect, and when

12

she inadvertently sat on a sheath and began waddling about the room with a dozen portraits of Lincoln pasted to her ass, most of the class broke out into laughter. She wheeled on us.

'I suppose y'all find this funny?' she fumed.

For some reason, she assumed Trip was behind this outburst. She stormed down the aisle and hovered over him, pretending to try and remember his name from the roster even though it was obvious she knew who he was: everybody knew who he was.

'Perhaps you can tell us, Mr . . . Ware, is it? Under what circumstances can I mail a package second class?'

Like a magnetic unit, we swivelled in our seats to watch. I think we all understood this was some kind of direct challenge to his public stature. To everyone's surprise, Trip seemed to visibly falter. He sank down into his chair and we watched his face turn a terrifying crimson.

In that electric silence, a sudden bravura came to me.

'We all know one thing . . . !' I called out.

The whole class turned in my direction. I pointed at the stamps on Miss Mackie's ass:

'. . . you're gonna need a lot more postage than that to get it there.'

By the end of that day I was a hero. I could feel kids buzzing when they passed by me. I stood at my locker thinking, *the ability to laugh and owning a sense of humour are distinctly separate things*. Then, from nowhere, Trip's hot bulldog breath was on my face.

He hauled me toward him.

'You think I cain't fight my own battles?' he seethed.

'I'm sure you can, Trip,' I said. Instantly, a crowd materialised. Here we go again, I thought.

'Damn right I can,' he said. His starched collar was so close it cut into my chin. I could smell its factory newness.

13

In a blur, his fist shot toward, then past my face. I felt a tug at my neck and realised he was inspecting the inside label of *my* shirt, as if subjecting me to some kind of veterinary examination.

'Wash and wear,' he announced to the crowd and shook his head pathetically. 'Your momma pick this out for you?'

This was a cue for the onlookers to laugh. Thankfully, that seemed enough for Trip and he slammed me against the locker and headed down the hallway.

I bent down to pick up my books and then slumped to the floor. *What was it about these kids?* It seemed that everything that meant anything to them could be bought in the perfectly ordered piles of menswear at Tate-Browns Clothiers.

Which was where I went.

I had plenty of cash from my ongoing insurance scam. I'd been keeping it in a shoebox in my bedroom, thinking perhaps I would order a full set of Topps baseball cards. I'd already blown ten dollars on a US Meteorological Service weather balloon advertised on the back of *Jughead* comics. The balloon had promised to be forty feet in diameter. I began to doubt that it would ever be shipped, and when it finally arrived it turned out to be some sort of oversized whoopee cushion with urinary applications printed on one side.

Now, I wanted to conform, to be accepted by this crowd. I think I realised Trip and his insults were manipulating this idea, but I was just sick and tired of feeling exiled.

Tate-Browns had an oaken atmosphere that made it seem almost like a museum. The shirts were luminous under small green-shaded lamps. I traced my finger across the high thread counts, each one a crisp talisman. I would unfold one, try it on, examine myself in the mirror, and set it aside. Unseen hands would then spirit it back to its resting place.

The manager observed all this with gathering disdain. Finally he approached me.

'You buying or just wasting time?'

'I can assure you, sir, I intend to purchase something.'

'These shirts are all too big for you. These are *men's* shirts.'

'I'm good for the money if that's what you're thinking.'

'I've had it up to here with you goddamn kids. You come in here, paw over the merchandise and send your daddies back to settle up.'

'I'll have you know, sir, my daddy is Admiral of the Pacific Fleet. One more word from you and I will have this place subjected to maritime law.'

I'm not sure where this brazenness came from. Like I said, I think I was just fed up. I slapped a wad of cash on the counter and walked out with a blue Gant traditional button-down with stayed collars, size 14½.

I wore the shirt to school every day. My head poked out of the aperture like an emerging larva. The other students perceived this as some sort of snide burlesque, and did not take me seriously.

On a late November night my mom notated her departure with a pair of zippery tyre ruts right over the septic tank that, no doubt, had been stinking up her life. I woke up in the middle of the night and heard my dad yelling into the yard, then the screech of tyres tearing away. I went outside. He was standing in the street in his worn bathrobe, a pint glass held cautious and level, determined not to let the incident cause him to spill a single drop.

'She'll ruin the goddamn gearbox she drives like that,' he said, listening to the car grind off into the night. 'Mark my words, she'll be calling us from some fillin' station in an hour.'

To me this implied she was going a long way away.

'What happened?' I said.

'She blubbers and gets fed up,' he said. 'I've seen all this before.' He turned and went back inside, and I followed. A Roger Miller record was skipping on the phonograph. *Woman would you weep for me.*

'Is this about money?' I asked.

My dad looked surprised.

'How can you ask such a thing?' He gestured briskly around the room as if to demonstrate all the marvellous possibilities he'd lavished on her. A deformed couch. A battered trestle table on which sat a souvenir whisky bottle in the shape of Governor George Wallace of Alabama. A shiny standing ashtray that flushed cigarette butts down a trapdoor.

'Have I not provided?' he said. 'Tell me, what's missing?'

He said this genuinely. I marvelled at how my dad could just make things up and instantly believe them.

My mom's departure infected the house with a kind of dormancy. Dad was present in the most minimal way someone could accept. He couldn't even make my school lunch properly. I would go to school, open my lunchbox and find a selection of briny bar snacks: pig's knuckles, pickled eggs, beef jerky.

'How are you getting along with *Roget's*?' he asked me one afternoon. We were in the living room.

'I'm still in the A's,' I answered.

'You haven't even cracked it open, have you?'

'I just said . . . here . . . *apex, appurtenance . . .*'

'And their meanings?'

16

'I don't quite know yet. It doesn't matter. The people I use them on don't know what they mean either.'

He shook his head and sighed expansively.

'That you have more pressing interests, Richard, I've no doubt. You're what, twelve, thirteen? Go on. Have a high old time. Meet up with your buddies, possibly even girls at this point . . .' He waved his free hand with a gesture that suggested he knew all about this from experience. 'But sooner or later you are going to understand the value of an uplifting conversation. And when I present you with a tool that will have implications for your livelihood many years down the road, you are to treat it with respect. Are we clear?'

I'm making more money than you, I thought to myself.

'Yes, sir.'

'You need to start applying yourself. Your mother was not suited to putting up with spectacular failure on your part.'

'Wait a minute. You're making it sound like it's *my* fault she left.'

'She walked out on *both* of us, kiddo. Don't forget that.'

The school year advanced. There were cotillions, scholastic fetes, winter carnivals, each with specific fashion caveats. Reputations seemed to be made or ruined by these events. When a kid named Grey Kimball was spotted in gym class wearing calf garters to keep his socks from wrinkling, word rocketed through the hallways. By week's end, garters were a mandate. Rumpled was bad, creased was good: one's status lay within that spectrum. Gant introduced a line of paisley-patterned dress shirts that briefly divided the school into viciously opposed camps, shattering lifetime friendships. No one seemed to be able to come to an agreement on cashmere sweaters. I couldn't help but view these kids telescopically. I suppose I was in awe of them. They seemed better at their world than I was at mine. And each day, when Elise Alderman would pass me in the hallway with indifference, I felt completely foreign, like something giving off a bad smell in a perfect room.

After a few months of domestic limbo, my Aunt Anne showed up on a sanitation crusade. She was a maternity nurse who I always kind of appreciated for the fact that she had a V in her upper teeth large enough to actually get her cigarette through. She set about cleaning our tiny house with an alarming fury, scouring the dishes as if she meant to erase their patterns, stabbing a cloth into the house's dusty surfaces with a vengeance that clearly affirmed her disgust with my dad. I sat in a chair in the living room and watched, fascinated.

When she was done, she pounced down on our battered couch.

'You want me fix you something to eat?' she said.

I told her I was okay.

She dug her fingers up into her scalp and undid something that caused her bun of hair to unravel: a kind of declaration of work's end. The room was dark in the late afternoon with only the blue-grey light of the television to highlight the dust still filtering through the air. She threw a cigarette into her teeth, where half of it immediately disappeared.

'Lord love a duck,' she said.

'What?'

'What? The goddamn stock exchange. Who do you *think* I'm talking about? Your father.'

There was a stack of insurance brochures on the trestle

18

table. She picked one up and thwacked it with a thumb and forefinger.

'You know these are worthless, don't you? That's just like him.'

'They *are*?'

'My God. He sends one to your Uncle Roman and me every Christmas. I had a series of lumbar spasms here a while back . . . tried to collect on it.' She waved the policy emptily. 'They sent me back a letter that was like a seashell. You opened it and you could hear them laughing. Where, by the way, did you get that ridiculous shirt?'

'Never mind. Does he know they're worthless?'

'If he doesn't I'll eat a bug. Your father is very quick to notice things and very slow to do anything about it. For example, your mother is due back any day now . . .'

'You *talked* to Mom?'

'I don't need to talk to her. She's my sister. She'll come back because she's very thorough that way. The point is, what will your father do to correct the sordid state of affairs around here?' Having sanitised the house, she now appeared to be giving my parents' marriage some kind of medical scrubdown.

'She will not put up with his drinking for ever,' Aunt Anne said, then lowered her gaze to impart a dire prognosis. 'Next time, she'll go for good. She'll leave him drunk and alone. As, eventually, will you.'

I wasn't sure I liked where this was going.

'And the sad part is, he'll be all right with that. No, that's not even the sad part. The sad part is there'll be no one there for him to say that to.'

'Say what to?'

'That it's all right with him.'

I think I was a little confused now.

'What does all this mean to you?' Aunt Anne asked.

I thought about telling her that this was just part of an ever-expanding nightmare. That between home and school life I was merely a smudge between two vast nothings. That I wished desperately for a return to a normal life. I wanted my mom back home, in her normal state of belligerence. I wanted to be at a school full of normal kids who played baseball, masturbated, picked their noses and couldn't care less what they wore. These were desires I could not easily convey to my aunt. So I just said:

'I wish we'd move again.'

I buried myself in the thesaurus. Words suggested a way to grow out of myself, to reach some new rendezvous. I would stare at columns of synonyms as if they were stacks of coins that might eventually amount to a true currency. And to ply this currency I joined the debating team, where, in short time, I faced off with the team captain, Elise Alderman.

Here I held a chance of equal footing. We stood ten feet apart, bolstered by lecterns, bandying concepts way beyond our reach. The world is round. You are to affirm or negate this, our moderator instructed. I was handed an old Ptolemaic map for reference. Really, I thought, flat, round, egg-shaped . . . what difference does it make?

'A tall mast appears before the ship's body,' stated Elise.

'In an *allusory* sense it is flat,' I announced.

'Allusory?'

'In that everything eventually disappears. My mom, for instance, has vamoosed. She may as well have fallen off the earth.'

'Digression!' yelled the moderator, but I went at it. *Agnostic, abnegate, aver, avouch, affirmate* . . . I had no idea what I was saying. I just launched these words like grapeshot, hoping to create electricity, to make an impression on Elise.

Afterwards, she lingered in the debating room while I gathered my coat.

'What was that all about?' she asked. Her startling blue eyes scrutinised me.

'I don't really know. I just signed up to avoid going home.'

'Well, you're in way over your head.' This made me think of Trip Ware.

'How's your boyfriend?'

'Trip is Trip,' she said cryptically. Before I could consider what that implied, she changed the subject.

'What bands do you like?'

'The Allman Brothers. Marshall Tucker. Creedence. What about you?'

'I like Creedence,' she said.

'Even though it's misspelled.'

'What?'

'Creedence.'

She looked at me strangely and then realised it was true, and it felt for just a moment as if we alone held knowledge of some tiny cosmic flaw. I sensed an opportunity and reached to take her hand. She didn't move to pull it away. She stared down at the floor awkwardly and I found immeasurable joy in this. When she looked back up at me, I went for it. I could tell right away that she didn't know much more about kissing than me. I attempted something with my tongue. Feeling the hard clamp of that Erector Set wired to her jaw, I could imagine what Trip had been up against all summer. It was like trying to push Jell-O through a keyhole.

Finally she pulled herself away.

'Wow,' was all I could say. To my immense relief, *wow* seemed perfectly acceptable to her.

21

'Well, Richard Hall,' she said. 'It was very nice to meet you again.'

The air in the room seemed to be heaving. Possibly it was my own life expanding. I stared at her for as long as I thought I could get away with it. Her face started to turn red. *What a feeling!* Then she turned and walked out of the room, pausing by the door,

'There's only one *e*, right?' she said, brightly.

'Right!' I shouted back, far too loudly.

Then she was gone. Come Valentine's Day, I decided, I will give her my thesaurus. We will spend hours together deepening our relationship, lying at fingertip proximity poring over new and exciting words together. *Wow,* I thought again. And all the synonyms for *wow* as well.

I walked home that afternoon by the usual route: through Myers Park and then through my own tatty, fortified neighbourhood. When I passed the tavern, I could hear my dad inside, braying demonically at some unseen accuser.

'Don't *you* tell an Airborne Ranger when he's had too much to drink! *Only an Airborne Ranger* knows when he's had too much too drink!'

I went inside and found him on his bar stool, veering wildly. He patted the seat beside him, indicating I should join him.

'New bartender,' he informed me, motioning to an unfamiliar guy behind the counter, then yelled in his direction, 'What the hell do you put in your hair!' The bartender looked like he'd had just about enough. My dad had a kind of wayward look on his face. Then he started in.

'You strike up a conversation with a fella, you're thinking *I've seen this guy before.* But you can't place him. When the moment avails itself you show him a

22

policy. He says, *I've seen this policy, pal. I bought one of these policies from you.* Is that a fact, I say. He says, *In fact that is a fact.* He says, *This policy wouldn't buy a raffle ticket on a jaybird's ass.* I don't mind telling you, I'm flummoxed. Surely a mistake has been made. And before I can even offer up a reasonable explanation, he's out the door, stiffing me for the bar tab. I go there to the payphone, put in a call to Lowell, Massachusetts. I make appropriate enquiries. I am informed not only is the company out of business, they are being dunned by the Better Business Bureau.' He stopped to sip his beer and collect himself. 'Shysters, goddamn shysters. She's home, by the way.'

'Mom?'

'Who else?'

'What did she say?'

'Who?'

'Mom! What did she say when she got home.'

'She said, 'Who's hungry?' and started in on the kitchen.'

'That's great,' I said.

'Indeed it is. I really missed that car.'

'Let's go home, Dad.'

The bartender looked relieved. He came over and presented the tab.

My dad stood up unsteadily and waved his hand imperially over the empty glasses in front of him, trying to make them disappear. He patted his pockets like an old comedy routine, indicating no money.

'My livelihood, sir . . .' he said to the bartender, 'is imperilled . . . Don't pretend you haven't been listening to my story.'

'I have money,' I said and pulled out a nest of bills. He eyed the money and then me with what looked like several conflicted thoughts. Finally he plucked out the required amount of singles and spread them across the counter, a glacial transaction clearly meant to goad the bartender. He took my arm and I walked him out. We headed up Brandywine toward home and my mom. It was late winter and a strong cold breeze had come in, running the smell of our house straight out of town.

Everything takes time, I thought, and wondered why that was such a wonderful revelation.

impact

PETE GRAHAM MEANS to *impact*. He's just started up his own ad agency, Snakebite. Snakebite has landed its first account: a small European supplier of fish fingers.

'I'm sat with the client,' he is saying. 'The client says to me, "Pete, I have a modest budget." I say, "No. Modest won't do. You'll take me on because you want to *impact*."'

He's a big ruddy fellow with a face full of broken capillaries, always dressed for some wonderful idea from the night before that he can't seem to remember. He's got that kind of enthusiasm that makes you think of an aerobics instructor.

'I can see the client is clueless,' he continues. 'I indicate beyond the office glass to the plant. I say to him, "What do you see out there?" He says, "Fish fingers . . . what do you see?" I tell him I see perch modules teetering along tracks, speeding through various processes of automation, a humming, tinkling chorale of perfectly flaked and cubed fish product. I tell the client I'm sorry, I cannot sell that any more than I can describe the colour red to a blind man. What I can sell, I tell him, *what I can sell* is *Tasty. Fresh. Convenient.* These are things you cannot touch. I can sell the fish finger *experience.'*

'What a load of shit,' I say

'Of course. That's advertising.'

'But you got the account.'

'Indeed I did.'

He catches the barman's eye and signals another round. I'm pretty sure he's half-in-the-bag now. He tells me he's got two hundred square metres of open-plan space in Charlotte Street, zinc worktables, a *shit-hot* graphics team, two dozen employees.

'What I do not have,' he sighs 'is unity.'

'Unity?'

'Employee unity. A sense of teamwork. The gestalt of the competitive landscape.'

'Well, it's early days yet,' I answer. *Early days? Did I just say that?* Lately, Briticisms have been creeping into my vernacular. *Filthy day. At the end of the day.* British forward thinking ends at sundown. They just want to *get through the day* so they can start drinking. But then, come to think of it, so do I.

Pete stares up at a stuffed exhibit in the corner of the pub: a moth-eaten badger poised mid-pounce over a dilapidated grouse. When he gazes back down at me, it's with the same look as the badger, a look that effectively traps me.

'I want you to teach them softball,' he says.

'Softball?' So *this* is what he's invited me here for.

'I've entered Snakebite into the Ad League.'

'I've never coached softball. I don't—'

'Yes, but you play it.'

'That doesn't mean I—'

'I want to win the league. Worst to first, that sort of thing. I think that would congeal us into a workforce. I expect you can work wonders.'

Ad League is where I'd first met Pete. His former agency had a team and he'd inducted me as a ringer. These were jovial, unstately gatherings, basically just an excuse to drink beer. No one except me really seemed to want to take it seriously, and after single-handedly turning a triple play and getting nothing more than a perfunctory 'cheers for that' from a teammate, I'd decided to stop playing.

Pete reaches down and retrieves a large cardboard box, which he sets on the table: a gross of T-shirts.

'This gets our name out there,' he says, holding one up against the late-afternoon light. The shirts are a lurid red with a coiled rattlesnake on the front. 'What do you think?'

'Can any of your employees *play* softball?' I ask.

'None of them have the first clue,' he answers, then adds somewhat mysteriously, 'but Sanjeev in accounts is a Bengali.'

'Meaning?'

'I'd imagine he's a keen cricketer. That's a start.'

'Cricket isn't softball.'

'Nonsense. It's like the difference between hair and fur.' He hands me a sheet of paper. 'These are the league tables.'

'*Schedule*, not tables. It's called a *schedule.*'

'If you say so. Anyway, your first match is next Wednesday. Now if you'll excuse me, I have to make it to Hertfordshire in forty-five minutes if there's any chance of nailing my wife.'

Pete leaves me with the T-shirts, and just like that he's off to *impact* on his wife.

I have observed professional baseball coaches all my life: unsmiling men full of small dismissive gestures, alternately expectorating viscous liquids and scratching their genitalia. They take the game seriously. It is this taciturn approach that I will use to shape Pete's team into a winning unit.

The following day I have a hangover like nobody's business. We assemble for our first practice in Regent's Park at the footbridge, in the shadow of the Great Mosque. The park has a quality that makes it seem endless and tightly manicured at the same time. In the distance the BT Tower dominates the horizon. It is a hideous-looking thing, a bedpost covered in bottle caps. Overhead, low rumbling airbuses compete for the ruination of the British skyline.

Such splendour seems lost on the Snakebiters: seven guys, four girls, all looking irked and vaguely listless, like they've been forced to attend mandatory CPR training.

Various introductions are curtly exchanged and I have a chance to assess the components. There is a Julius. A Barnaby. A Hamish, a Humphrey, a Raynor, a Sanjeev, a Roderic. There is a Hermione and two Fayes. These are not names remotely associated with athleticism. I need guys named Whitey, Deke or Chipper to win at softball. Frankly, it's dispiriting. Three of the guys have clearly arrived straight from work. One is wearing a suit and dress shoes. Of the four girls, only one, a tall, pretty brunette, Sam, looks fit. But she is, at that very moment, constructing a giant spliff. The other three try to look invisible, their faces suggesting impending flight. Sanjeev from accounts is in cricket whites.

'There were supposed to be fourteen players,' Humphrey explains, 'but two got sacked from the agency this morning. And Jez Gyngle's gone for beer.'

'Fair enough,' I say. 'Well, first things first.' I pull out the T-shirts and distribute them. You would think I was handing out *I'm with stupid* shirts.

'Oh my God,' drones Hermione.

'These are hideous,' says Faye One.

'And they're one-size-fits-all,' I answer, trying for cheeriness.

'Do we have to wear these?'

'Absolutely. Your boss insists.'

'Well, *I* just don't think it's necessary,' says Faye Two.

'Neither is advertising,' I say, because, frankly, I've already had enough. This invokes an immediate cold silence.

'If we're going to play like a team we're going to look like a team. Let's go.'

I heave the equipment bag on to my shoulder and head toward our assigned field. The Snakebiters straggle behind glumly, like remoras trailing an old shark.

They are gathered at my feet at the base of a towering plane tree, a somewhat biblical panorama. I toss a softball up and down, feeling its heft in my palm, a feeling that connects me to a million childhood memories. Skills, I have decided, will come later. First I want to impart a reverence for the game itself.

'Base. Ball. Base. Ball. There are ten positions. Learn them. We observe the opposing batter. Is he left-handed or right-handed? This dictates in which direction he will likely hit the ball. We make adjustments in our positions.

We stay aware at all times of the base runner. Is he standing at first? If so, we make the play to second.'

They all look around at each other, trying to make a joke of this with facial expressions. One young man rolls his eyes, runs his fingers down the length of his tie and makes it snap.

'The ball cracks off a tubular shaft of cold-rolled aluminum at a velocity exceeding sixty miles per hour. Common sense dictates that you dive out of the way. That is a natural response, but that is not the game of softball. You use a large padded mitt to stop it. You keep the mitt between your body and the approaching ball. That is what protects you. The alternative is severe bodily bruising, possibly even brain damage. Learn to trust your mitt.'

They are all in shock. And scared. Good, I've *impacted*.

'Softball,' I explain, mellowing my approach, 'is quite simply about going home.'

I place the rubber pentagon – home plate – on the ground and put my toe to its edge.

'This is home. You can see it's even shaped somewhat like a house. In this respect, the game might be viewed as a sort of pastoral journey.'

A relieved murmur ripples through the crowd. If you want to appeal to Brits, invoke home. *At the end of the day,* Brits love to be home, *snug and cosy*.

Just as quickly, I lose them again.

'Naturally, this means *we must not allow the other team to get home.'*

'Awwwww.' As if I'd just said, *kill the homeless*.

'*Hey!* Your social opinions are without merit here. Christ, half of the world thinks you people are pansies when it's really only an issue of playing the right sport. Now I am going to assign a line-up.'

Robotically they stand up as one and arrange themselves into a queue.

'No. No. No. A line-up is the players' positions. There are infielders and outfielders. The outfielders stop the balls that get past the infielders. The infielders protect the bases. The infield is in the shape of a diamond.'

Then, with what can only be described as classic British truculence, I get this:

'Why?'

'Why what?'

'Why is it in the shape of a diamond?'

'I can't begin to comprehend what's behind that question.'

'Certainly a triangle makes more sense.' As one, the Snakebiters agree on this, as if it's been an oversight of baseball for the last 150 years.

'You know what? You're absolutely right, and as soon as I get back to the States I will take that up with the Commissioner of Major League Baseball. But for right now, let's just go with a diamond.' *Take me now, Jesus.*

I lay out the bases. *They are too far away,* complain the Snakebiters. *Can we move them up a bit? Must I stand in front of the batter when I bowl? Surely it's safer to stand off to one side.* At one point there is the following supremely withering exchange:

'All right, Barnaby, is it? You mind if I call you Barney?'

'Please don't.'

'Fine, Barnaby, you pitch.'

'Do what?'

'Pitch.'

'*Where* on the pitch?'

'Sorry?'

'Where on the pitch do you want me?'

'No. The pitch is not the field. The pitch is when you throw the ball.'

'Oh, you mean bowling.'

'Bowling . . . right. But it's called pitching. If the ball is over the plate it's called a strike. If it's not over the plate it's called a ball.'

'When is a ball not a ball?'

'When it's a strike. It's only a ball if it's a wide pitch.'

'I thought you said it was a field.'

Also:

'Sanjeev, it is not appropriate to stand in the outfield and run up to deliver a softball at supersonic speed. You must stand in one place and lob it underhanded.'

Then, a horrific display of fielding ineptness. I stand at home plate with the bat, throw the ball up and pepper it in the general direction of the infielders. They collide with each other, a delirium of limbs moving in unnatural directions. They react with horror-movie histrionics when they either catch it or don't catch it. Within fifteen minutes they have thoroughly lost interest. They stand around in a kind of rapture thinking about . . . well, not being here. By the tree, behind home plate, the young man named Hamish is pressing himself against one of the Fayes, mashing into her face while extending his glove. Meanwhile, the right-fielder Julius, one of Pete's shit-hot copywriters, is on his mobile phone, conducting a surreal conversation:

'. . . Okay, now delete the sentence that ends with *enhanced flavouring.* Okay. Delete *Norwegian* and replace with *cold North Sea* . . . sorry, replace *cold* with *icy* . . . and in the last paragraph cut the following phrase: *inviolate territorial waters.*' A series of hard grounders passes unimpeded through his legs. 'And cut the entire sea shanty, except for the first two lines . . .' Later a ball is sent flying over his head and rolls into some undergrowth. Julius goes to retrieve it and does not reappear, but eventually texts the pitcher to say he cannot find the ball.

The twelfth man, Jez, arrives with a crate of beer. Instantly my formation dismantles and descends on him like a pack of coyotes. There is almost a scuffle to get at the beer. Out of nowhere, a group of Nigerian youths invades the outfield and takes up an impromptu football game, swarming back and forth like aquarium fish. Hamish and Faye have slyly disappeared to the far side of the sycamore. All I can see is Faye's elbow, near the base of the tree, moving back and forth in a kind of pneumatic way. It is springtime.

And that's when I beaned the imam. It was an accident, of course. Smacking a Muslim holy man in the face with a softball is not the sort of thing they do in Britain. It happened right after one of the girls had discovered semen in a baseball glove, just when it seemed things couldn't get worse. I only meant to hit a sharp line drive at the Nigerians, as a way of moving them along. But the ball glanced off my bat and rocketed toward a park bench near the third base line. The imam was sitting there minding his own business, no doubt lost in some impenetrable Islamic reverie. It caught him square in the nose and he went over like a sack of flour.

I ran over there to see if he was okay. To this day, I don't know why I didn't put the bat down beforehand. I just wasn't thinking. I had to push through a cluster of park-goers who had already gathered. The imam lay sprawled on the pavement, his great cloak fanning in all directions. He looked strangely docile. Blood was streaming from his nose but his hands were at his chest, clasping the Koran, as if it were some kind of jet pack that any second now might transport him skyward toward Paradise. This was a very unnerving tableau, and if anyone had bothered to truly study the grainy camera-phone photographs that would appear in Arab-language newspapers the following day, they would have seen that the man with the baseball bat standing over him had a look of genuine *concern* on his face.

The following day, Pete summons me to his agency in Charlotte Street. His office is on a stainless-steel gallery overlooking the work floor. He is at the window waiting for me, his wide-spread hands up against the glass. He looks like one of those tree frogs. I have to walk through the open-plan work area where the Snakebiters avert their eyes, pretending not to see me. I'm going downhill fast.

Pete opens the door for me and I follow him in. There is a man in a keffiyeh seated beside the desk, his hands patiently folded in his lap.

'This is Ibrahaim,' says Pete. 'Ibrahaim is with the Muslim League.'

For just a moment this is confusing. Pete reads it on my face.

'The Muslim League is not remotely interested in playing softball. Ibrahaim is here to help mediate this unfortunate situation.'

I offer Ibrahaim a handshake. He merely nods back at me.

'You are gracious to have come,' he says.

I take a seat in one of those flimsy Danish chairs that's just a chrome frame and leather strips and feels like an ass hammock. Pete looks pretty rattled. His mouth is a restrained mark, like a *Peanuts* character.

'How's the imam?' I ask.

Pete's eyes shoot toward Ibrahaim for a response.

34

Ibrahaim informs me that the imam has lost two litres of blood and has been fitted with a protective face shield that he will have to wear for two months.

'Al Jazeera led with it on this morning's broadcast,' adds Pete, who's always right on top of the New Media thing.

'Please convey to the imam that I'm truly sorry,' I say.

'I will certainly do that,' says Ibrahaim. 'But I feel it is more important that you convey those sentiments to the imam's followers.'

Pete shows me a couple of Arab-language newspapers: my picture and an accompanying story.

'What do these say?' I ask Ibrahaim.

'The stories say the imam was the victim of an accident and was attended to by helpful passers-by.'

'That's good.'

'But the picture says something entirely different. The picture shows a man with a bat attacking the imam.'

'We both know that's not what it appeared.'

'Unfortunately, that is *exactly* as it appeared,' says Pete. 'This is the kind of picture that extreme elements of the Muslim community will exploit. They will sell it as an anti-Muslim *experience*. Isn't that right, Ibrahaim?'

Ibrahaim nods slowly. 'Perhaps.'

'So, what, is there going to be a fatwa on my head?' I joke.

Ibrahaim doesn't think this is a joke.

'That is a very naïve statement. You seem to be confusing the Nation of Islam with the Mafia.'

I look out the window into Charlotte Street. It is a wonderful spring day, dampened only slightly by the sheer discomfort of this meeting. I point out that this whole thing could have been avoided if the Royal Parks had had the foresight not to put park benches down the third base line.

'That's why it's called the *hot corner*,' I add, somewhat gratuitously.

Silence.

'Okay,' I say. 'How do I apologise?'

'It is not possible to apologise,' says Ibrahaim. 'What's done is done.'

It is moments like these, when I'm accused of setting off the Third Crusade, that I tend to get a little defiant.

'What do you want from me then?' I bark. 'It was an *accident.* You act like I rubbed the damn softball in pork before I hit him.'

There is another long, frigid silence, after which Pete remarks:

'I'm fairly sure that was unnecessary.'

'Perhaps you need to explain to the Muslim community how the game is played,' says Ibrahaim. 'Then they would understand how this accident occurred.'

'You want me to explain to a billion people how softball is played, when I can't even explain it to those eleven pissheads downstairs?'

Pete looks disoriented.

'You must calm down,' says Ibrahaim. 'We are trying to bring unity between Muslim and Christian communities. That is our sole aim . . .'

'*Unity* . . . By the way, Pete, I'm done coaching your team. A decent third baseman would have snagged that ball.'

'What if you just explained the nature of the game?' Pete offered. 'What you told my players.'

'I don't remember. I was hungover.'

'About going home. Softball is about going home.'

'Yeah. I told them that. I should have gone straight to the rules instead of some soppy analogy.'

'It is an excellent analogy,' said Ibrahaim. He stood up, to give his next words magisterial weight.

36

'Many of the world's problems would cease to exist,' he said, 'if Americans would simply go home.'

The last-minute ticket from Heathrow to JFK cost me a fortune. I actually cracked a joke about it to the guy wedged into the seat beside me.

'They charge you an arm and a leg and there's still not enough room!' I said cheerfully. It was a crap joke, but at least I was getting my sense of humour back. I already had a stiff Bloody Mary on the tray in front of me and we hadn't even pulled back from the gate yet. My seat-mate, a large black man in a matching golf cap and sweater from a St Andrews pro shop, reacted with a look so surly I actually found myself checking to make sure he wasn't minus an extremity or two. I just needed this bad-luck streak of miscues to be over, and it wasn't until the plane was over North America and I looked down at the patchwork of baseball diamonds cropping up from the outreaches of Long Island that I could truly feel anything like euphoria.

rachel

YOU REALLY HAVE to wonder how it's all going to turn out for today's youth. Used to be kids respected your private property. Nowadays, I don't know why, but there seems to be some kind of idle hostility between teenagers and adults, nothing to do with age, just a small plain hatred awaiting transmogrification into sinister acts of wanton destruction. The Wife has a more laissez-faire attitude about it. 'Let teenagers be teenagers,' she says. Well, that's her motto, not mine. I'm all for forced internment, Guantanamo-style.

When our fifteen-year-old daughter Rachel threw a party, 2,300 of her MySpace friends showed up and did over $450,000 worth of damage to our home. The Wife and I had gone away for the weekend. We do volunteer work for those orphaned burros you always see advertised in the back of the Sunday supplement. We returned on a Sunday evening to find lighting fixtures ripped from the ceiling and urine-soaked carpets. A hallway closet door featured the splintered outline of a hurled body, fully splayed like a cartoon silhouette. Someone or something had violated our cat.

The incident set off a collective buzz around our small town and made both the *New York Times* and *USA Today.* Rachel was duly shamefaced about the whole thing, especially when she became the focus of derision on a couple of late-night TV shows. Funny thing, these teenagers: it's all 'look at me!' until you end up as a sketch on *Saturday Night Live.* The Wife felt that embarrassment at the national level was probably sufficient punishment for Rachel, but I still felt I had to put a fatherly stamp on the whole thing, so I banned her from going out of what was left of our house for a month.

'Some of these kids are not your friends,' I tried to explain to her. To show she wasn't upset, she went to her room and hacked into the Pentagon, cancelling several lucrative arms contracts. The Wife informed me that hacking into the Pentagon was a well-known thing hysterical teens did. Nonetheless, I got a nasty visit from some government types who advised, in no uncertain terms, that I'd 'better line that little Bathsheba out real fast'.

During her month of forced confinement, Rachel collected an additional 135,000 friends, an act that quite clearly implied some sort of Bulk Retaliation. I am not painting Rachel as an ugly child, but as a troubled kid who never used to do stuff like this.

I replaced the ceiling fixtures and laid brand-new wall-to-wall carpet, consoling myself that the place had needed it anyway. I hung solid-core doors in the hallway to repel anyone's attempts at human perforation. The Wife was visibly delighted with the makeover, even if it *had* been forced on us. To celebrate, she had a few guests over for an indoor salmon bake: the Sloans, the Peaveys and the Ginyards all showed up. She also allowed Rachel to invite a few MySpace friends over. This was done behind my back and when 6,400 of them materialised I was steamed beyond belief.

'Rachel's still on probation,' I fumed.

'You ought to ease up on her,' the Wife replied. 'She's only fifteen. Besides, have you ever tried *talking* to her friends?'

'Why?'

'You might find they're not as uncommunicative as you think. Help me with the plates.'

I decided to put her little notion to the test. I wandered into the living room, where a few hundred kids milled about listlessly. I approached a young man in an oversized hooded sweatshirt who, at that particular moment, happened to be jetting a six-ounce can of lighter fluid across our new couch. I made a stab at small talk with him.

'You don't mind me asking,' I said, 'why do so many of you insist on misspelling the word "ludicrous"?'

He regarded me blackly.

'Ludacris. You mean the hip-hopper?'

It had not registered with me that Ludacris was an actual person.

'Clarify hip-hop,' I said, perhaps a bit too stridently.

'Come again?'

'I know what it *is*, but what exactly does it *mean*?'

'Hip is the attitude. Hop is the moves. Ergo *hip-hop*,' he answered, then struck a match.

'Well,' I said, trying for conviviality, 'sounds like this Ludacris has all his bases covered!' I leaned forward and blew the match out. The kid went sullen and receded into his hood like some kind of legume, a snap pea maybe.

As for the salmon bake, there wasn't enough tableware to go around and it took an almost biblical approach to carving to see that everyone got fed. We all sat with paper plates on our knees. Wanda Peavey, aware of the frosty atmosphere brought on by 6,400 surprise guests, chirped blithely about how much the new decorations really 'jazzed' the place up. I couldn't get over the fact that my position of Home Rule had been usurped by both Wife and Daughter, and when another MySpacer, a dreadlocked whippet with a look of permanent gastric distress on his face, stood up and asked where the toilet was, I told him, in a voice heard by all, to make himself at home and pee on the new carpet. This got a steely reprimand from the Wife. On the plus side, our cat, Judge Kennesaw Mountain Landis, seemed back to his old self, at one point retrieving a dead sparrow from the garden and delivering it to Rachel's feet, a gesture that for her, at least, seemed to denote a certain amount of water under the bridge.

By October, things had quieted down considerably. The Wife and I went away on a three-day weekend, this time to eastern Nevada to build some wintering sheds for feral mustangs. Goddamn if Rachel didn't throw another MySpace wingding. Though she would later swear the number was only 45,000, some of our more reliable neighbours' estimates were well into six figures. Regardless of how many showed up, the assholes burned the place to the ground.

The Wife and I stood there amongst the smouldering, acrid rubble and watched the last of three hook and ladder trucks – having done all they could do – drive away. A few brazen MySpacers had actually stuck around to watch the place roast, as did a lot of neighbours, which made for some palpable tension. The pack instinct, so to speak, was on alert. I think I felt a little of it myself because I suddenly found myself line-tackling one of the sonofabitches, sprawling him to the soaked ground, his face registering a kind of effigial surprise. I tried to explain to him in so many words that his suave and malicious disposition could only hinder him in the future, that arson was not the be-all and end-all he viewed it as now. All this while driving my knee firmly into his Adam's apple. In these days of Instant Messaging, I suppose my little one-to-one assault probably struck some as a laughably puny gesture, but goddammit, I was peeved. A couple of volunteer firemen had to pull me off the kid. Rachel, incidentally, was nowhere to be found.

Afterwards Larsen Snipes, everyone's local insurance agent and all-around Johnny-on-the-spot, took me aside. Larsen's a real straight shooter. He suggested I cut my losses and leave town. I conceded his point, but told him I wasn't giving up that easily. The following day I got a letter from Allstate informing me my premiums had quadrupled. That the letter was addressed to a house that no longer existed seemed almost existentially funny, and for a fleeting moment made me wistful for my own teenage past and its careless enthusiasm for ruining lives.

After a few days it was apparent that Rachel had gone AWOL. The Wife, of course, was distraught. She phoned the police, carefully describing Rachel's various tattoos, piercings and last known items of dress. The police assured us they were as eager to find Rachel as we were. I kept picturing her cowering somewhere, mortally ashamed, afraid to come home, suicidal even.

We'd checked into a Best Western out by the overpass. We never left the room, ordered pizzas in, jumped each time the phone rang, waited desperately for a development.

It came in the form of primetime evening news. A throng of MySpacers had ransacked a neighbouring town, torching the high school and the mayor's house. We watched the footage on TV, recognised a number of faces. None of them was Rachel's.

After that, the wildfire effect kicked in. MySpacers reportedly descended on a place called Fort Riley, Kansas, and left nothing standing. They commandeered a crude oil tanker in Puget Sound, stranded the crew at Vancouver Island, then ran the whole thing aground near Ukaleet Island, Alaska, leaving a 200-mile oil slick. In California, 40,000 of them ramraided the home of someone named Avril Somethingorother and forced her to perform unplugged. Halfway through they walked out en masse requesting a refund. In a large Midwestern city they purchased a Major League Baseball franchise and promptly unloaded all the quality players. Their actions turned increasingly unpredictable. A T.K.Maxx store reported that MySpacers had poured in and 'actually cleaned the place up'. The Wife and I scoured each pixel, hoping for a glimpse of Rachel. We felt helpless, each event like a wave washing our precious daughter further out to sea.

Throughout this ordeal our good neighbours remained stalwart. The Ginyards and Peaveys visited constantly, armed with pot roasts and Tupperware offerings, insisting that we come stay with them until we got back on our feet. If there was any bad feeling toward Rachel, it was politely suppressed by all. Everyone wanted to see her back in the fold. Wanda's husband Ray, who ran his own driving school, told us he had all his instructors on daily lookout. Estelle Ginyard, who's perhaps a bit too fashion savvy for her own good, told us she was positive she'd spotted Rachel, 'wearing North Face', on the oil tanker in the news. Her husband Gary, who happened to be staring out the window at that moment, said that couldn't possibly be true, since he was actually *looking at her*, huddled beneath the overpass, not fifty yards from our motel room.

She'd been there, it turned out, for five days. She was hungry and dishevelled and her eyes rimmed red from crying. I'm not a religious man, but I silently thanked God she was alive, then fought a rising urge to tie her to a very large boulder and drown her.

'I'm glad it's you who found me,' she said, sniffling. 'Mom must be a wreck.'

'We could only imagine what you were going through,' I said. I didn't know who I meant by *we*, except that I thought it was in the air that it had all gotten a little out of hand and she needed to know she was still in the public's good grace. Then she poured herself out:

'I'm not the stoic you think I am, Daddy. This MySpace thing, it gets under your skin. It's a business and it wants all of you. You don't see that until it's too late. You're allowed to be anything you want, your most intimate details, truths, fictions, exchanged at the flick of a send button. There's no social awkwardness. Do you understand that, what it's like to be so effortlessly popular? No, of course you don't. As your list of friends expands . . . so does your obsession . . . your obsession with the power to win friends. The power turns ugly but by then it's too late. You reach a point where you don't know if you're a part of the list or the list is a part of you. You realise you need to meet these people, to see if their friendship is genuine. Good sense tells you not to arrange clandestine meetings, that there's safety in numbers. So you invite *everyone.* How was I to know it would turn into the rape of Nanking?'

I have an almost terror sometimes of Rachel's stupidity, but in that vivid moment, shivering in her sleeping bag, beside the frigid river running under the bridge, she was transcendent in her vulnerability. There was nothing for me to say. I put my arm around her and she rested her head on my shoulder and we sat there together and watched the river, like time itself, pass by.

We bought a house in the country, one of those river-rock-façade things that everyone was putting up a few years back. To be honest, I was excited. Town was in-undated with McMansions and crystal meth anyway. A rural retreat sounded exactly that. I had formulated a vague theory that maybe the closer one was to nature, the fewer proclivities for Pure Evil. I had Rachel's future in mind. The new house overlooked twenty-three acres of pasture. Occasionally coyotes came into the yard, scrawny things, displaced by recent homesteads. They seemed to stand for some faraway era. The Wife took to throwing them table scraps from the deck off the side of the house.

As for Rachel, I lowered the boom. No more parties, period, and she could put that in her hat. I told her to thin her roster of 'friends' to a manageable level . . . no more than 6,000 . . . that *then and only then* she could invite a few over.

When they did start coming around – limited to handfuls of twenty-five or thirty, tops – they seemed noticeably less threatening. Gone were the city kids with their straight teeth and rich bulldog faces. These kids moped about, cheerless waifs whose uniform hairstyle, jet black and pitched at a very severe angle – this being the sticks – gave way to a mullet at the back.

'What's with Rachel's new friends?' I said to the Wife one night. 'They all look like Leonard Nimoy.'

'Rachel's gone emo,' she replied.

I did a bit of checking around and learned that *emo* constitutes some nether-strata of teenage affectation that advocates 'not being afraid to show one's feelings on the outside'. This is achieved by wearing a lot of what my grandmother used to call 'pancake foundation'.

Rachel, to her credit, stayed out of trouble. Mostly she and her emo pals just sat around listening to dreary music and making small incisions in each other. At least the house wasn't on fire.

circadia

WINTERS IN MONTANA do weird things to people. The wind kicks up, the blizzards create isolation and perma-dark and events take on a kind of distal quality, as vivid and self-contained as a series of snowscene paperweights.

I was at a friend's party, a raucous, bourbon-soaked purging of the cabin fever that all Montanans succumb to by mid-February. I was standing in the kitchen, drunkenly aloof, when a fellow who'd been eyeing me from across the room sidled up. He reeked of woodsmoke. I figured him for one of those types who lives alone in a cabin full of antlers. He could have been forty, could have been sixty, it was hard to tell behind the scrub brush of facial hair. He had the penetrating grey stare of a Weimaraner. Without bothering to introduce himself, he pushed his face up to mine.

'There's a difference,' he announced, as if it was his

final word on an argument, 'between light and reality.' I played it safe and nodded agreement, avoiding eye contact.

There followed a long, meandering discourse on his perception of 'reality'.

'Life,' he said, 'is how we interpret the silence around us.'

He talked about silence for a good half-hour, beyond the point where it was convenient to amble off. I just had to stand there and indulge his cosmic wittering.

I felt a little sorry for him. No one else at the party seemed to acknowledge him and it occurred to me he'd probably just crashed the gathering to escape the cold outside. He said his name was Russ. He said he was a part-time locksmith. Then he said he was dying.

'How's that again?' I said.

'A year from now I won't be here.'

'What's wrong with you?'

'Cancer, I reckon.'

'You *reckon*? What kinda cancer?'

'It's non-specific. All I know is, it's eating away at my gut, and I'll tell you something else: I'm shit-scared.'

'Jeez,' was all I could think to reply. I suppose that explained his quasi-existential blathering, a fella desperately trying to grasp the enormity of his demise. No time for small talk when you're dying of non-specific cancer. I resigned myself to hanging out with him the remainder of the evening.

'Let's us meet up tomorrow,' he said when I was leaving. 'I gotta ask a favour of you.'

He tore a corner off a six-pack carton and scribbled some directions: 89 North to the old grain elevator, right on to an unpaved road, two miles to the first house on the right.

I didn't want to meet up with the guy. Ever. But like I said, I felt sorry for him.

* * *

50

Next day, I drove out there. It was high scrubland that gradually rose to the foothills of dazzling mountains called the Crazies, though in the encircling grey of winter you just had to take the land's word for that. I turned on the radio and listened to the morning man out of Bozeman solemnly relating the world's miscues. There was an ongoing environmental dispute over a reclaimed palladium mine near Deer Lodge. An elk had gone berserk in a high school parking lot in Gardiner and chased after some drum majorettes. The girls were refusing to return to class. Highway 89 was drifted over with fresh snow, the sky was low and leaden and foreboding and the world had a kind of spectral quality that made me think that the announcer and some traumatised majorettes and myself might be the only people on earth.

Russ's place sat in a brace of bare cottonwoods, ghostly candelabras that seemed to be floating in abstraction. There were a few outbuildings and a long drive sloping up from the road. The house itself was small and chaste-looking, covered in cedar shingles.

I knocked on the door and no one answered. I knocked again, then tried the lock. It was open and I went in.

'Russ?'

There was no answer. I was in a kitchen, which was plain and spare and void of any homely curios other than a magnetic Billings Mustangs baseball schedule on the fridge door. I studied it for a moment. The image of ballplayers had an unseasonable effect, like when you suddenly smell suntan lotion the wrong time of year. I opened the fridge, helped myself to a beer, then wandered through to the living room.

There was a wood stove hissing in the corner. The low winter sun made the only light in the house and I wondered about his priorities. If I were dying would I scrimp on indoor lighting or say to hell with it and fire the joint up like Vegas? It was impossible to view anything in the house without seeing it as temporal. Here was a dying man's wood stove. Here was a dying man's sofa, a dying man's coat hangers on the floor, a dying man's closet door opened, revealing a collection of snap-button shirts and cowboy boots with curled-up toes, as if already announcing his corporeal departure.

There was a .38 Special lying on the coffee table. Not unusual for Montana, but not something that goes unnoticed.

I sat down on the sofa, instantly aware of being watched. I turned slowly to discover a deer studying me through the living room window. After a moment it faded from sight and I reached into my pocket and pulled out a pen and notepad. I wrote a note, put it on the table and weighted it down with the butt of the .38: *Stopped by. R.*

'What are you writing?'

I looked up to see Russ staring at me as intently as the deer I'd just seen. For a second I thought of shamans, shapeshifters.

'A note,' I said. 'I couldn't find you.'

'You wouldn't happen to have any Milk of Magnesia, would you?' he asked.

'No. Sorry,' I said.

'I didn't figure you'd come,' he said. The darkness of the room threw shadows across his face that made him seem just as sombre and unreachable as the night before.

'What was it you wanted, Russ?' I asked, feeling uneasy. *Milk of Magnesia?*

He came around the sofa and sat down beside me, lowering himself cautiously. Then he picked up the .38 and turned it over in his hand.

'When I go,' he announced, 'I don't wanna linger. Don't want the indignity.'

He let the weight of the gun rest in his palm, then offered it to me.

'I'd appreciate it,' he said, 'when the time comes, you put me out of my misery.'

'What?'

'I ain't got the nerve to do it on my own.'

'Why me?'

'Cause you ain't too close to take it that personally.'

In a way, this made sense: I could see a kind of compassion to it. But no way was I going to agree to this. Instead I asked him where the can was.

'You gonna wet your pants?' he asked.

'Possibly. This is a very unusual request.'

'It's down the hall. Then I want you right back here.'

I got up and went to the bathroom and closed the door behind me. There was a dead bolt and I pushed it through and sat on the toilet seat wondering where to go from here. Then I heard him outside the door.

'All you gotta do, when the time comes,' he explained, 'is put the gun in my hand, squeeze my finger over the trigger. Then let yourself out the door.'

'Christ, Russ. I'm trying to have a piss in here.'

'You better open up. I heard you lock it.'

I looked around at my options. There was a window above the sink big enough to crawl out of, but I figured I wouldn't make it to my truck before he caught up with me again. I didn't hear anything for a while, and then I flushed the toilet absently and put my ear to the door to see if he was still there. Suddenly his big brushy face appeared in the white void of the window. He threw it open. The bathroom turned instantly frigid and I could feel his frozen breath in my face.

'You're wonderin' how many others I've asked before you,' he said.

'Not at all. I'm wondering why, as a locksmith, you never lock anything around here.' This washed right over him.

'Everyone I know who's died of cancer, they went out the hard way,' he said. 'If it happened to you, would you opt for a short cut?'

'I don't know, Russ,' I said, and that was true, I'd never really thought about it. 'But if you don't come back inside you're gonna freeze to death and this whole discussion becomes pointless.'

'That a joke?'

'No.'

The face disappeared. I unbolted the lock and shot out of the bathroom and went back to the living room. The gun was on the table. Then I heard the stomp of feet in the kitchen doorway. He came in trailing waffles of snow and went to the wood stove to warm his hands.

'*Every life is precious,*' he said. 'Ain't that what all them born-again Christians like to say?' He turned and walked up to me. 'So if life is so precious . . . how come they have to be born again?'

'Beats me, Russ.'

'Well I'll tell you this . . . life ain't all that precious when you're sprouting tubes on a hospital bed, your ass hanging out of some stupid gown, waiting for the Angel of Morphine. Fuck that.'

I reached down and picked up the gun.

'Fine, Russ,' I said and put it in my coat pocket. I wasn't implying anything. I just thought it was a prudent idea to get it away from him.

I promised him I'd think about it. I wrote my phone number on the notepaper, made the 7's inconclusive so they might be mistaken for 1's and got the hell out of there. All I needed to do now, it seemed, was to avoid him the rest of my life.

When I got home, I hid the gun on a basement closet shelf where I keep my gopher rifles. A mouse shot out from the darkness, hurling past me in a startling blur. I moved my gun-cleaning kit aside and discovered its nest: a cache of mattress batting and deer sweetfeed that it must have dragged in, kernel by kernel, from the garage. I turned and saw it sitting on its hind legs in a corner, glaring at me, like I owed it some kind of explanation. I killed it, using the butt end of a .22 Ruger: just smashed it, basically. Instantly, I regretted it. It didn't even try to get away, just sat there, its tiny black eyes accepting the imminent blow. In that moment, I pictured Russ.

The winter churned on. I began to doubt the encounter with Russ had ever occurred.

The Owl is my local haunt. It's an appropriately ill-lit bar, with a TV at one end constantly tuned to sports. The owner, Dana, has been known to turf everyone out when the Knicks blow a lead. When this occurs, he locks the doors and starts blasting 'Milk Cow Blues' from the stereo. We all have to stand outside on the pavement and wait for him to cool off and let us back in. I went there one night to meet up with some friends. The Knicks had the night off and the atmosphere was fairly placid. Figures darted through the front door furtively, mindful of the frigid air they were letting in, and we'd all turn to see if we knew the faces buried in fleece or fur. That was when I noticed Russ. He was sitting by himself near the door, cradling a whisky glass, eyes staring out from that black brushy face like dying coals.

'Does anyone know that guy?' I asked.

Everyone at the table looked. There was a murmuring of consensual non-recognition. Then a girl named Tilda, who was somebody's near-girlfriend and a nurse and a newcomer to the area, said she did.

'Wacko, wacko, wacko,' she announced in a kind of marching cadence. She seemed a little drunk.

'Does he have cancer?'

'I don't know if he's sick or not, but he's hopeless. He came on my ward a few months ago. Enteritis, something like that. They told him he needed to go to Billings and get checked out. But you know how you talk to some people and you can just tell you're not getting through? He wanted to talk about the Egyptian pyramids. He kept going on and on about how the number of blocks corresponds with the solar cir-whatchamacallit. It was the night shift, no man's land. I went down the hall for some B12. When I came back he was sitting on the bed whacking one off, devil-may-care.'

'Oh my God,' said a girl beside her.

'It got worse. He asked me if I'd pee on him. Just like that. *Could you pee on me?* Like a kid asking for an Oreo.'

We all reserve a kind of diffidence for out-of-staters until they've proven themselves. I think we silently agreed this particular remark reconciled Tilda to our community.

'Oh my God,' the girl said again. 'What did you do?'

'What do you think I did? Had a couple of interns show him the door.'

'You didn't call the police?'

'Of course I didn't call the police. I'm a nurse. Besides, you never know when you're going to need a locksmith.'

She held up a bourbon glass like a chalice and stared through it, assessing him.

56

'He's got too much hair to have cancer,' she concluded, and that was that.

The conversation shifted and I sat there and considered how trying it could be to live in a small town where you had to work hard to be accepted. Acting crazy could just be a way of avoiding social rigours. I got up to go outside for a cigarette. I walked past Russ, avoiding eye contact. Just as I reached the door, his arm shot out and grabbed the bottom of my coat.

'How are you, Russ?' I said.

Without gravity, without looking at me, he said, 'We still got that deal?'

'Sure thing, Russ.'

'Then I guess I'm okay.'

That night, I had shivery dreams: me coaxing his waxen finger on to the trigger, squeezing lightly. It occurred to me that maybe I should leave, move to another town.

On a day in March the sun re-emerged. The blue sky seemed like a rebirth, and I decided to return the .38 to Russ. I knew if I wished to continue living in my home town, I needed to confront him as a means of keeping him at arm's length. I got the gun from the basement and drove out to his place. The last two miles up to his house was an almost impassable skating rink of black ice and skid patches. I drove at a crawl. There was a view of the Crazy Mountains so deliriously majestic that I wondered if I was travelling toward sunniness or sunniness was travelling toward me. But when I turned in to Russ's place, the pervasive brilliance evaporated. His house looked terse and final, the wraithlike cottonwoods bracketing it like quotation marks around a single word: dread.

*   *   *

'I figured you'd turn chickenshit on me,' he said. We were in his kitchen. He was barefooted, dressed in some kind of loose-fitting beachcomber pants and a Homer Simpson T-shirt. 'So I made alternative plans.'

'What's that?' I asked.

'An Intra-ethical Drug Delivery System, slightly used, from eBay. It administers morphine at timed intervals.'

'Good for you, Russ. Here's your gun.' I laid it on the kitchen counter.

'Should be here any day now.'

I reached in my pocket and pulled out the bullets and laid them next to the gun.

'And I would appreciate it, when the time comes, if you'd help insert it into my scrotum.'

'I thought the pain was in your gut.'

'It moved.'

'They have hospitals to do that.'

'I can't go to the hospital.'

'Because the nurses won't pee on you?'

'Arguing this is depriving me of my dignity. I am a putrid collection of failing components. I would appreciate a little humanity.'

'I don't believe you have cancer.' I said, staring him straight in the eye. 'My best guess, Russ . . . is you're lonely. Maybe you have trouble networking. But count me out of your drama.'

I walked out and he followed me.

'Suit yourself, but I'm gone in the next reel!' he called out, like a petulant child.

He stood in the snow in his bare feet, watching me escape to my truck.

'I knew all along you'd pussy out!'

'It's a beautiful day, Russ!' I called back, and it was. The landscape was a meringue of gleaming white. I paused at the door of my pickup to take in the view. All of us know we're going to die, but none of us wants to believe it. We'll refute it till it's irrefutable. Maybe Russ did have cancer, but I'd chosen to think he didn't and the sheer gorgeousness of the day backed me up. I looked down the road and caught sight of a UPS van struggling uphill in my direction, brown and haunched like a lone buffalo. In that moment my resolve faltered. Would this be Russ's morphine device? What then?

I decided to know.

I walked down to the bottom of the drive and stood there waiting. If the package *was* for Russ, I would carry it up to his house and hand it to him. In Montana, this is what we call *neighbouring*.

While I waited, I looked around to take note of the other houses on the road. There were only three as far as I could see. Across the road, set well back along a stream bench, was a farmstead surrounded by hulking green John Deere machinery. Further up, a redwood split-level thing with a pristine barn and an orderliness that no doubt signified retirees, and beyond that – a good half-mile or so up the road – a stone monstrosity of vaguely Quakerish dimensions that seemed to be trying to compete with the scenery and losing. I noted these residences as a way of gauging Russ's surroundings. I wondered if his neighbours knew him and what they made of him.

The van was still a quarter-mile down the road. I watched it enter a bend by a stand of broad cottonwoods where the low winter sun squeezed it into shadows.

Then something comical, almost otherworldly, began to unfold. Occupants from each of the houses, having bundled themselves up against the cold, were trudging through drifts to meet the van. I guess they were *all* expecting packages. This was a lottery and there was only going to be one winner.

When everyone had reached the end of their respective drive, we waved at each other to complete the joke, then stood there in our little clouds of frigid vapour. The progress of the van was so cumbersome I think we all must have felt guilty about subjecting the driver to such an ordeal. When the van emerged from the shadows it was jerking dangerously toward the road's edge. I watched for it to right itself but it didn't. As if in slow motion, it wallowed off into a defile that ran alongside the road and lay there beached, half submerged in the snow, tilted at a crazy angle.

I was the first to reach it. I got the door open, and as soon as I looked in I knew the driver was having a heart attack. He was wedged upright against the far door, perspiring wildly, his pupils wide as nickels, like someone watching a movie from the front row of the cinema. He was buried beneath bundles and overnight envelopes and I climbed in and started clearing them away, chanting, 'Take it easy, fella, just take it easy' in a kind of stupid mechanical way.

A small black heeler appeared, running tight circles around the truck, and moments later, its owner: a rancher with a big red face.

'What do you reckon?' the rancher huffed.

'He's having a heart attack. I know the signs.'

'Don't this beat all,' said the rancher. The two of us managed to lift the driver out and prop him against the side of the van, like some kind of roadside shrine.

'Can you walk?' the rancher asked him.

'I'm coming out of my skin,' the UPS man announced and started to slump.

I'd heard something or other about a 'golden ten

minutes' in these events, and told the rancher we needed to get the guy inside somewhere warm and comfortable and call for the EMS. I indicated Russ's house, which was nearest. The rancher crinkled his red face.

'No one's home,' he said.

'A guy named Russ lives there.'

'Oh he's there all right, but trust me, no one's home.'

We went there anyway. The two of us made a kind of chair with our hands and got the UPS man up the long drive and into the living room, where we laid him out on the couch. I told Russ we needed to use his phone. He said he didn't have one. The UPS driver pointed to his own jacket pocket and I reached in and found a phone and dialled 911. The dispatcher told me to ask him if he carried nitroglycerine pills, otherwise sit tight and wait for the ambulance.

Eventually the other two neighbours arrived: a rangy younger woman in vivid Lycra running-wear that made her vaguely resemble a superheroine. Her name was Laura. She was followed a few minutes later by an older woman whom I actually recognised: a retired hairdresser, Sandra somethingorother, who puffed in with a slight look of disappointment like she'd just come fourth in an Olympic event. To our fascination, the UPS driver lay on the couch gurgling and making strangely apologetic pronouncements.

'I've never taken up more room than I needed,' he groaned. His voice sounded larval and distant.

'Until now,' said Russ.

We all looked at each other for clues to Russ's belligerence. It was obvious he considered this gathering an incursion. Sandra assumed the role of host. At one point she attempted to turn on a wall switch to illuminate the room. Nothing happened.

'Your bulb's out,' she said to Russ.

'What do you want me to do about it?' he replied.

The rancher, whose name it turned out was Dean, was clearly uncomfortable and made a big gesture of going off to get his tractor to plough the road to accommodate the ambulance.

'Why? Is that what Jesus would do?' Russ said sarcastically. Dean gave him a chilled look that said, *I'll deal with you later.* When he'd left, Sandra offered to make coffee for the rest of us.

'What do you think this is, a truck stop?' said Russ.

Sandra and Laura disappeared into the kitchen. I was alone with Russ and the UPS driver.

'Here we are,' Russ said.

'Yeah, Russ, here we are.'

'How do you feel?' he said.

'What do you mean?'

'They say Death comes in threes and here we are. How do you feel?'

The two women returned empty-handed.

'No cups,' said Sandra, looking straight at Russ. He shrugged emptily. The room took on the air of an awkward vigil, especially when out of the blue Russ said to the UPS driver, 'Why don't you hurry up and die?'

'Beg your pardon?' the driver whispered.

'You heard me.'

'There's no call for that,' said Laura.

'Look who's talking. I see you runnin' by my house every day. Maybe you think you're cheating death, but it makes your tits sag like clown shoes.'

'Well I'm done here,' she said. She swept past us and into the kitchen. The UPS driver was watching all this unfold, his mouth gaped open, eyes like white holes. He slowly lifted an arm and studied his watch. 'Will this winter never end?' he said hoarsely.

I followed Laura out to the kitchen. I felt the need to apologise to her, though I wasn't sure for what.

'For what it's worth . . .' I started

'What's *wrong* with that horrible man?' she asked.

'I honestly don't know. Some people get a sense of power out of being baffling.'

'What is he to you? Friend? Relative?'

'Neither, actually. It's a little complicated,' I said. 'Maybe I'll explain sometime in better circumstances.'

'Maybe I don't really wanna know,' she said and left.

I stared out the kitchen window and watched her break into a jog. She turned downhill at the end of the drive, heading toward the UPS van, where Dean's tractor sat idling. She joined Dean in rummaging through the van. After a while they went off in separate directions, empty-handed.

Sandra came into the kitchen and drew herself a drink of water from the tap. She looked rattled.

'That no-good sonofabitch . . .'

'Russ?'

'. . . just verbally raped me. He told me I was frittering away my creek allotment on a pointless garden. I told him I am entitled to three inches per deed contract and thank you very much I will use it as I see fit. Is there anything around here to go with this?' She waved the glass at me, a prompt to look for something alcoholic. 'Also what business is it of his anyway?'

'This isn't the time for petty bickering,' I said. There was some whisky on a shelf above a built-in desk and I went over and took it down. She grabbed it from me and twisted it open.

'I think he has a serious case of Seasonal Affective Disorder,' I said.

'Here's a non-clinical assessment,' she answered. 'He's an asshole. Do you know, not a single light works in this place? *Who lives like that?*'

She downed the hooch in one, waited for it to make its long drop and shivered slightly at the desired effect.

'Tell you what, Sandra,' I said. 'Go home. I can handle this until the ambulance comes.'

She didn't seem to really want to go. She set the glass down on the counter and this time poured a straight shot. I suddenly got this strange sense of something missing, something out of place.

'You only need the broadest courtesy to be a neighbour out here,' she was saying. 'When I arrived twenty years ago the place was full of alcoholics, degenerates, trout-fishing bums. In fact I managed to slide one to the altar. But that one,' she said, indicating the living room, 'takes the door prize.'

Then it hit me.

'Where's the gun?' I said.

'What gun?' she said, looking around confounded.

'There was a gun on this counter . . .'

I took one step toward the living room, heard a shot and felt cordite singe my nostrils. I went in and saw the reclined UPS man limply waving the .38 about, like a baby with a rattle. Russ was performing a kind of sailor's jig, arms akimbo, trying to position himself in front of its trajectory. I lurched for the couch and snatched the gun from the driver's hands. Russ stopped gyrating and pulled himself upright with a look on his face like someone had just shut down the disco mid-song.

'Sit down, Russ!' I said. I might as well have been scolding a puppy.

He grinned back.

'Or what, you'll shoot me?'

'No. I will bust you in the mouth.'

'No you won't. You'll announce it over and over but in the end you won't do a goddamn thing.'

Sandra had trailed in to watch, agog with horror and fascination.

'He's too crazy to beat up,' she assessed. 'What he needs to do is go up to Warm Springs and get himself certified.'

'Sandra, do me a favour,' I said. 'Go down to the van and see who that package is for.'

Eventually the ambulance made it up the road and we got the UPS man away. Russ's behaviour toward him had no doubt had a defibrillative effect. He looked genuinely elated to be getting out of there. Sandra retrieved the package, which, it turned out, *was* for Russ. It was square and weighty: quite possibly the purported medical device. I felt supremely conflicted. The fact that he had actually tried to get himself killed made me think he'd been telling the truth all along: that he was terminally ill and desperate. For all the trouble he'd created, I ordered him to unwrap it in front of us. This he did, slowly and deliberately, and in a way I felt like I was facing up to my own mortality.

It turned out to be a collection of connoisseur porn: *Shaved Asians Volumes 1–4*.

Spring appeared as a series of false stuttered thaws and then erupted blazingly, all pinks and greens and hay fever. I found myself thinking back to my first encounter with Russ and his ruminations on light and reality. I realised right then that it literally had been a cry in the dark. So one day I drove out there and dropped off a carton of factory-fresh 60-watt bulbs on his kitchen porch.

One night in June he came over to my table at the Owl, looking tanned and fit.

'What happened to the cancer?' I said.

'Musta passed,' he said, then eyed the girl I was with: not a girlfriend, but getting there.

'You with him?' he asked her, right in front of me. Later I saw him trying to slip her his phone number.

I'd run into him in the street. He'd announce he'd been working out. Said he could bench-press his own weight. He'd ask me about girls I knew.

'We should get together, hunt some pussy,' he would say.

I still have the gun. I'm thinking of calling him up and asking if it's still okay to come over and shoot him.

a binding agreement

EPPY CLONINGER, PART of that current generation of magpies who accumulate information rather than knowledge, had never been able to find an ideal girlfriend, someone shapely, alluring and uncomplicated: like those chrome silhouettes you see on the mudflaps of semi-trucks going down the interstate. He'd look at a woman like that and think, *I bet she doesn't have a needy bone in her body.*

He'd had his share. Ones who cooked and ones who didn't, ones who would sit on top of him and do Sudokus at the same time, ones who sold cosmetics in department stores and came home every day reeking of a different product, ones who, like Eppy, claimed to be putting everything they had into the relationship but really just wanted to go back where they came from. And *every one of them* ended up being too goddamn needy: high-strung, jealous, moody . . . to him it wasn't right. He was diligent and rock-chalk faithful. He hated the thought of hurting anyone. As far as he was concerned, women were more sensitive than a five-dollar condom and he deeply respected that without remotely understanding it.

His last girlfriend was Miriam Locane. They had a nice courtship, unremarkable in a small-town kind of way, moved in together and for a while everything seemed possible. But eventually her insecurity got the better of her. She would ask him point blank, 'Do you love me?' and he would reply, 'Yeah, sure,' without embellishment. He wasn't so dim that he didn't understand that that question required a lot more, but he felt helpless at espousing his true feelings. He'd been raised by Calvinists, too literal-minded to be emotional.

'You act like just *having* a girlfriend is enough,' she complained.

'I just said I loved you, didn't I?'

'You don't get it, do you?'

Maybe he didn't.

Sensing she needed something in the way of a romantic sacrament, he attempted a poem. It started out from the heart:

> Fortunate me
> Such elemental luck
> That you bring out the old man in me
> Or is it the future child?

And that was it: all he could think of, all he felt he *needed* to say. He worried that it wasn't exactly text-heavy. Bereft of further self-expression, he logged on to the computer and searched some Google outposts until he came up with a string of gibberish that seemed close enough to poetry.

Still alive, setting buds for another season
I came from Nashville with my opulent
Trouble finding the right chord progression
NOW YOU CAN
Radiate what u consider to be ur mass

That night they went out to a vegetarian Chinese restaurant and he presented her with the ode, working it in between the tofu dim sum and the sharkless fin soup. She clasped one hand to her chest and held out the other to him before she'd even finished reading it. Eppy felt eminent relief. He had been banking on the fact that the gesture was more significant than the actual words.

'It's lovely,' she beamed. 'Kind of free associative, isn't it?'

'Yeah,' Eppy answered, hopeful that this would return the relationship to a level of pleasant detachment. When they got home that night she banged him with new-found vigour.

It wasn't enough, of course. Miriam purchased an expensive-looking scrapbook and – making sure he was watching – lovingly inserted the poem under clear plastic like a delicate leaf. The bulk of the remaining pages suggested to Eppy more work to come.

'I love it when you're relaxed and spontaneous,' she said a few weeks later, a less than subtle hint that the scrapbook awaited further contribution.

He waited until she went to bed and then hit the laptop. He tried to think of two words that might off-handedly be associated with romance. He decided on *promise* and, for some odd reason, *meadowlark*. He Googled *promise meadowlark*. There was a lengthy distraction in which he found himself perusing the life and career of Meadowlark Lemon, the famous Harlem Globetrotters basketball player, then a foray into a Find-a-Classmate site where he attempted to discover if any of the kids he had despised in high school were dead. Eventually he decided it wasn't worth the 29.99 subscription price to find out.

Fourteen pages in, he found what he needed.

Silvery notes of gladness improve your credit score
Meadowlark Lane
Pepper Pike, Oh
Summer videos promise of the ataris.
Ataris promises
living in an atrium
New event invasive species shows
promise

Miriam was slightly confused but nonetheless thrilled with it.

'What's that mean, *Pepper Pike, Oh?*' she asked.

'Words that can't be put into words,' he answered.

That night she threw herself on him with such Olympian intensity he wondered if he would get through it with his spine intact.

To commemorate the deepening of their ardour, she purchased some extraterrestrial real estate. She sent off fifty dollars to a company called The Star Registry. A few weeks later they sent back a form letter saying congratulations, they'd found the perfect star for the two of them, and asked what they wanted to name it. Eppy opted for Gram Parsons, the tragically departed country singer. Miriam insisted on something more mutually meaningful: Schmoobie, her cringe-inducing pet name for Eppy. He relented. A star was born.

* * *

Eppy accepted that remorseless repetition was the basis for genial relations with girlfriends and dutifully searched the internet for more unheartfelt utterances. He usually wrote them late at night, scribing them on to high-quality parchment with a flowing felt pen, the only part of the process that required any true exertion.

On the third poem, he slipped up.

'What does this mean? *View as HTML*?' she asked quizzically.

Eppy took the poem and studied it:

. . . you illuminate with splendor for eternity. View as
    HTML
Jonquils turning toward the light . . .

He knew then he'd been rumbled.

'Did you get these poems from the internet?' she asked.

'They're not really poems,' he tried to explain. 'They're Google extracts that make me think of you.'

'What does that *even mean*?'

Eppy's eyes searched wildly around the room as if the cause of this discord might be somewhere else.

'. . . better words . . .' he said.

'Better . . . ?'

'Than what I could come up with.'

She started bawling. He made a dismal attempt to hold and comfort her.

'Oh God,' she sobbed, pulling away. 'You've *downloaded* your feelings for me!'

From there, her trust in him unravelled, manifesting itself as a period of plangent depression, then all-consuming disappointment. She became violently invasive about his past girlfriends.

'Who was that last one? Astrid? Did you trawl the internet for Astrid as well, Wordsworth?'

She said this with such unstinting bitterness that it seemed to Eppy she *wanted* to get worked up, to torture herself or something. He lied just to get off the subject.

'You shouldn't talk about Astrid that way,' he said. 'She was diagnosed as bipolar.'

'I thought you told me she got killed by a polar bear.'

'Yeah. That too.' He wasn't a good liar.

Eventually he reached the point any man reaches when he's been hounded too often. He thought to himself, *Well hell, if she's gonna be disappointed in me I might as well just go ahead and buy that giant flat-screen high-definition TV I've always dreamed of.*

He spent all his time in front of it. Maybe it was a way of shutting her out. There were the usual waterworks, shitfits, threats of leaving, and then one day she did. He wasn't happy about it, but the way he saw it, she'd brought all this on herself.

He went a long time without another girlfriend. Not for want of trying, but he was just a little gun-shy and also maybe his self-esteem was waning a bit. He was stuck in a rut at work. His car had 300,000 miles on it. He'd developed a mild eating disorder where he became afraid of trans-fats, and after that, saturated fats, and then realised he didn't know the difference between the two and kind of stopped eating altogether. He felt like he didn't have anything to offer women. He just needed his life to get a little better.

It got better.

He'd hooked his computer up to the big-screen TV and would sit at home and view his e-mails, which were ninety per cent spam, but, because they were so huge, had a kind of cinemascope quality to them. He also occasionally read those news bites they always had on the Google home page. Which was how he found out about Gliese 581-C.

The news headline said: *Major Discovery: New Planet Could Harbor Water and Life.*

The new 'super-earth', called Gliese 581-C, lies in the orbit of a diminutive red dwarf star located 20.5 light years away from Earth. Because of its relative nearness, Gliese 581-C could be a very important target for future space missions dedicated to the search for extraterrestrial life . . .

Alongside the story was a super-telescope photo of the discovery: the planet in the foreground and beyond that its star. The planet wasn't much to look at: pretty much your bog-standard galactic object. But there was something about the star in the background that caught Eppy's eye. He couldn't quite put his finger on it, but for some reason that star looked . . . well, *familiar*. Then it hit him.

He went to a closet and pulled out a big storage box and started rummaging through it. There were a lot of photos of Miriam and him in there, some ticket stubs from concerts and sporting events, the e-poems he'd written for her and a large brown envelope. He opened the envelope and removed the gilded gold certificate and accompanying drawing, and that was when he realised that he, Eppy Cloninger, *owned* the star that Gliese 581-C orbited: a star that was possibly essential to supporting extraterrestrial life. Put that in your pipe and smoke it.

Rather, he *co-owned* it.

* * *

'I knew if I lived long enough we'd run into each other again,' Miriam Locane said. They were at the Bark 'n' Beetle, an obnoxious Marxist health-food restaurant where everything came in the shape of a loaf. Eppy had already had a run-in with a squirrelly waiter who'd refused to serve two of the items he'd ordered on the same plate, claiming the countries they emanated from had 'conflicting ideologies'. Eppy pointed out that he didn't give a green goddamn about ideologies, he wanted mung beans and Tibetan yak cheese and he wanted them on the same plate, and if he sniffed so much as a milligram of trans- or saturated fats he would flip the waiter like an omelette.

'You haven't changed,' Miriam said sarcastically. 'Let me see if I've got this right. You can recognise a star twenty point five light years away, but you never noticed when I came home with my tips highlighted?'

Eppy tried to convey the excitement that astronomers were sharing about Gliese 581-C, that come June, its next transital pass-by, they'd be able to gather a lot more info about its make-up.

'Once a person gets away from you, they ask themselves, *How did I ever do that*?'

'There are some astonishing similarities to our own planet,' he said, ploughing through. 'Similar core density, similar axis wobble, possibility of multiple moons.'

'Moon. June. Look who's trying to come across all poetic. No wonder you stole all those poems.'

'Miriam, I am making a sincere effort to talk astronomy here . . .'

'Ha! Sincere? The only thing you ever did with any sincerity was bang me, watch TV, bang me, watch TV, bang me . . . Maybe one of your new girlfriends, one who understands what you're talking about, may warm to this conversation but I . . . and don't even try to tell me there's not other girlfriends, because I've been sniffing around and—'

'Miriam, will you *please* shut up and listen . . .'

But she wouldn't of course. She stabbed her fork into her salad and shrieked and blubbered in that way where Eppy was obliged to look around at the other diners and make some kind of apology with his expressions. The man at the table next to them scraped his chair back noisily and threw a napkin on the table as if to announce that he could not enjoy his Cashew Sunburst Surprise under these circumstances. Then Miriam started in on how she'd really had a hard time *healing* after the break-up, that it had been some kind of *inward journey* for her, and really, that was pretty much it in a nutshell, wasn't it, Eppy thought to himself, the whole man/woman thing: women were always on some kind of inward journey and men were pretty much up for any kind of *outward* journey, even if it was 20.5 light years away, which was why it wasn't really all that mindboggling that he could say something to his ex-girlfriend like 'I just think you and I should put these bad feelings behind us and come to some binding agreement on how we're going to handle this, because *if* Gliese 581-C *is* inhabited then as owners of its energy source *we're in the catbird's seat*: and even if it turns out the planet is composed of nothing more than just rock and water we're entitled to a share of the profits from metallurgical or hydrological exploration, not to mention the fact that any project undertaken to colonise the planet would have to pay us a sizeable users' fee . . .' but what *she* heard was 'I think we should get back together.'

tennessee basketball

T ENNESSEE WAS MOVING right to left on my radio and I'd practically pounded in my dashboard listening to the bastards blow the lead, get it back, then blow it again. This wasn't what you would call a stately game. In this part of the world, when Kentucky and Tennessee meet up, we take it seriously. The implications go far beyond the court. Every play, every score, every defensive stop occupies its own time and space.

I was driving a real shitbucket: an Oldsmobile Cutlass with no brake lights. If I wanted to slow down, I'd have to flash my headlight switch on and off manually so the guy behind me would think I was braking. I'd been meaning to get it fixed but I didn't have any money. The only thing in the car worth a damn was the radio.

The sun was just going down and, sure as their name, the Smoky Mountains were giving off a glorious blue haze. But whether or not this was a perfect day depended on the outcome of the game. The Cumberland River, high this time of year, ran along below me. Occasionally I spotted rafters in bright orange vests or a lone angler down there. There wasn't much traffic, which was good because most times you gotta be real wary on this stretch of highway. The goddamn lookie-loos in their SUVs and Winnies will slam to a stop any time they spot a family of bears wallowing in the roadside garbage cans. During tourist season, this road spits out corpses on a regular basis.

I came around a bend just as Tennessee got an uncontested lay-up to put them back ahead. I took my hands off the wheel and pummelled the headliner in elation and barely even noticed the pickup truck coming the opposite way. I might've drifted too far to the inside. We caught each other's wing mirror. There was a thump and the sound of ripping metal and for a brief moment the whole thing reminded me just how much of my life had been a failure: I can't quite put my finger on why. I slammed on my brakes and looked back to see the truck swerving crazily. It veered over into the opposite lane, overcorrected, crossed back and smacked into a guardrail. A fat plume of steam shot up from the hood and I cursed to myself. I didn't have insurance.

I thought about driving off. There was a time in my life when I wouldn't even have had to wait for the thinking music on that idea. But I'm toeing the line these days and the last thing I needed was John Law coming after me on a hit-and-run charge. They would waltz me back to jail for sure.

So I waited to make sure the Tennessee point guard nailed his free throws then I climbed out to check on the driver, and when I reached the truck, wouldn't you know, the sonofabitch had Kentucky plates.

The truck's motor was still running. I could hear a

broken fan belt slapping the underside of the hood and wondered why the dumb honyocker didn't cut the engine. There was some wire in the truckbed, smooth rolls and barbed rolls and a bunch of t-posts, so I figured him for a farmer. When I came up to the door, his window was down and I heard the game coming from his radio.

'What the hell just happened?' I said.

'Lofton just got fouled on a three-point play,' he said, staring at his radio. Lofton was the Tennessee forward, and whoever fouled him had just done about the most boneheaded thing you can do in a basketball game.

'You followin' this?' said the driver. He had a raw-knuckled face and a band of sweat halfway up his baseball cap. The hat had a Kentucky Wildcat logo on it. I'd learned in prison to assess people carefully, to appraise what you might get out of them. It's one thing to be observant and another to be wide awake.

'I am,' I answered. 'But from the opposite perspective.'

'Well, get in,' he said. 'This one's goin' down to the wire.'

I went around and climbed in. He had the radio loud to cover the sound of the slapping fan belt and I was thankful because it meant we didn't have to discuss the accident: whose fault it was and so on.

Tennessee went up by four and the Kentucky coach called a time out. The farmer turned the radio down.

'You drifted inta my lane. This much we know.'

I didn't want to admit that so I just kept my mouth shut.

'You against conversation?'

'No. I just didn't expect to be spending the afternoon listening to the game with a Kentucky man. You hurt or anything?'

79

'Nah. You?'

'I'm good,' I said.

'Well I guess we drew real lucky that way. You got insurance?'

'I do. But this is just a scrape. I can pay for the damage.'

He stuck his head out the window and looked back at my car. Then he shot a thin bolus of tobacco juice on to the road.

'You must think I just fell into the daisy patch,' he said.

'I'll give you my driver's licence. Send me the repair bill. I'm good for it.'

The farmer grunted and turned the radio back up. There was two minutes thirty-four seconds left. Tennessee had possession. You could hear the Volunteer band playing 'Rocky Top', the frenzy and cacophony of the home crowd mob braying for an upset. There was something about this notion – and the fact that the farmer was in hostile terri-tory – that made me think I had an advantageous position on him. We listened to the game and I was half putting an idea together in my head to get me out of this mess. Ramel Bradley sank a forty-foot shot from behind the arc for Kentucky and just like that the crowd went dead quiet. The clock was down to a minute and a half and then there was a time out and the game went to a commercial.

'I'll be right back,' I said and got out and went to my car. I reached into the glove compartment and took one of the stolen credit cards I'd been saving for tight spots like this: a Gold Amex. There was a near-full bottle of Knob Creek bourbon on the seat and I grabbed that as well. I opened it and took a long drink and, that quickly, everything was worthwhile again. My guilt was changing. I was thinking on my feet.

I went back to the truck and got in and offered the driver a snort.

80

He eyed me warily.

'Just 'cause you're a Kentuckian don't mean we can't be friends,' I said. 'You're gonna need this because your team is about to get whupped.'

'Won't happen. Tennessee ain't whupped Kentucky in one hundred and three years. Not in a championship game.'

'Anyone can have a bad century,' I said.

This almost got a chuckle out of the old boy. He took the bottle and put it to his lips, taking an amiable draw. He didn't even make a face and I knew right then he was a drinker.

'What's a Tennesseean doin' drinkin' good Kentucky bourbon?' he asked.

'It's my one weakness,' I said, and this time he really did laugh.

Tennessee had a one-point lead and inbounded the ball. This was a make or break play and we both stared intently at the radio. The farmer took another drink. The Tennessee guard appeared to be just standing there, pounding the dribble. There was every chance in the world my team was gonna fall apart – the way they always did – and I was getting agitated.

'Shit or get off the pot!' I yelled at the radio. The farmer cackled.

'Kentucky gets this one back and wins on the last shot,' he said, then suddenly: 'What I wouldn't give to be across the state line right now.' He handed the bottle back to me. A Subaru slowed up beside us. There were kayaks on the roof rack and two fellas inside with matching X-treme sport faces. They asked if everything was okay and the farmer waved them on impatiently. Right then Tennessee missed a fifteen-footer and Kentucky rebounded. They shot up the court. The announcer was

81

screaming at the top of his voice and we both leaned into the radio so close our faces couldn't have been more than an inch away from each other. I had the bottle tilted and a liberal amount of bourbon poured out on to the floorboard of the truck. The farmer didn't even notice. Kentucky drove to their own basket and scored with a half-second to go and just like that it was over. My whole world seemed to collapse on itself right then.

The farmer lurched back in his seat and let out a whoop. He grabbed the bottle from me and took a long victorious slug.

'This ain't your day, is it, friend?' he said, a little too self-satisfied for my liking. I was careful not to show any reaction. I just stared out the passenger window and listened to the pandemonium coming from the radio, feeling almost sick. When I looked back he was leaning toward me, his face suddenly red and aggressive.

'Now, what are you gonna do about hittin' my truck?'

I stared back, pretending to agonise over my answer.

'I'll drive to the nearest phone, call a tow truck and come back and settle up.'

'And I'm comin' with you,' he said.

'Your truck is half out in the road,' I said. 'You leave it like that, someone's gonna kill themselves.'

He thought about this. Then a strange kind of narcotic quality came into his voice.

'When my wife died . . . a couple years back . . . I said to myself, "I'm gettin' a dog." She never let me have one when she was around, didn't like 'em. So I went up to Hazard and got me this border collie I named Louie. He comes from seven generations of cow dogs . . . dogs that didn't wanna do nothin' but work and eat. And that Louie is maybe the best thing ever happened to me. I taught him *down, here, way to me* and *hold 'em* in one summer.

82

And he'll just stay on his belly and study you with his eyes until he's read you inside and out . . .'

The farmer paused to take another drink of bourbon.

'If he was here right now, he'd tell me in a second if you're worth a damn or not.'

I put the credit card down on the seat between us.

'Amex can do the same thing,' I said.

I left him with the bourbon and the stolen credit card and went back to my car and drove toward the nearest town. It was dark now with just the palest tip of sunset glowing behind the mountains. *I can't see Tennessee any more*: that's how I thought of it. I believed if I didn't stop and make that phone call, then I would never be any good and a fog of cowardice would envelop me the rest of my life.

I got to the outskirts of the next town. There were fast-food places and espresso huts and a large foreboding filling station bathed in so much vapour light it looked like some kind of sci-fi dreamscape and made me think that no matter how far into the future we get there's *always* gonna be Kentucky–Tennessee basketball and that's a rivalry that's *never* gonna go away. So I pulled in to the filling station and found a pay phone and called the police and told them I'd been hit by a drunk driver, that they could find him back by the guardrail right around the twenty-three-mile marker, and like I said, these days that ain't the evil kind of thing I do any more, but that sonofabitch had Kentucky plates.

werewolf of london

I saw a werewolf with a Chinese menu in his hand
Walking through the streets of Soho in the rain

THAT'S ME. *WEREWOLF.* I have a face full of fur and a substantial CV. I go back at least two thousand years, namechecked by the Greek and Roman mythologists, Pliny the Elder, Herodotus and St Thomas Aquinas. I am the subject of numerous legends, books, poems, movies . . . remember the one with Nicholson? I am one of the all-time great creatures of folklore and my question to you is: *Who exactly do I have to blow to get a quiet table around here?* Is that too much to ask? Just somewhere to lie low until this curse wears off and I get back to being my normal self, which is a normal man who lives in a normal tree-lined row of converted flats in a normal part of Chiswick and works for a normal publishing firm as a copy-editor.

All right, I say *curse*, but it's not like I haven't brought this on myself. Occasionally I enjoy drinking rainwater from the footprint of an animal. It's a kind of OCD. Some people can't pass a stop sign without licking it. Me, I drink from footprints. Unfortunately it turns me into a werewolf.

When this happens, I grab a cab straight for Soho, where I can blend in. Soho at night makes *Dante's Inferno* look like a *Where's Wally?* cartoon: a nonstop procession of alcopop-drenched cretinoids, lager-sozzled wage slaves, shrieking gaggles of suburban hen-party sluts in short black dresses looking like they're being swallowed by a mamba snake, forlorn shopping sociopaths with their accumulated Primark purchases, guttural Eastern European gangsters, louche pimps, skunkweed hustlers, neckless club bouncers with advancing foreheads, vaguely trollish cab drivers, gypsies peddling carcinogenic roses, grifters, drifters, thugs, lurid fluorescent drag queens, fluttering swarms of mosquito-like gays, gutter-crawling winos, the stagnant slime of a crumbling civilisation laying itself at the foot of an open doorway promising 'models' three flights up, into which a fat man in a bedsheet can currently be seen to enter, while nearby a businessman who really should know better sits chained to a streetlamp naked from the waist down spewing salmon-pink vomit down his tie like a volcano in its dying throes: a chunderous parade of human rodentia. And yet, *I'm the freak.*

As a werewolf *I am obliged* to mutilate someone, but frankly, I have such a low view of humankind – particularly on these streets – that I can't be bothered. If I'm going to eviscerate someone, there should be some ironic justice in it.

It's Christmastime. You can tell because of the festive display in the window of the sex toy shop: a Nativity scene constructed entirely from dildos, except for the Three Wise Men, who are butt-plugs. Those lovable Christians: such a plain and simple faith.

I can feel the ridges deepening between my eyebrows. I can feel my incisors sharpening and if I don't find a decent Chinese in the next five minutes I'm pretty much screwed, because once the claws come out I can never separate those crispy duck pancakes from each other.

I finally find Lee Ho Fooks and . . . this is the kind of shit luck I've had lately . . . they seat me upstairs next to the karaoke room. How am I supposed to enjoy my meal with some asshole ten feet away strangling the seventies?

By the time my main order arrives, I have to ask for a knife and fork.

'What's wrong with chopsticks?' asks the waiter, who's not even looking at me, but surveying the room for his next order. He's got that slack expression and robotic manner all Soho waiters display.

'In case you haven't noticed, I'm all paws here,' I say. He makes a big, bothersome deal of going off and returning with tableware, clanging it down on the table with distaste. I should rip his heart out right here, I think to myself. But I know I won't. It's my own heart that's just not in it. Then I pick up the fork and immediately it singes my paw. Sonofabitch if it isn't silver. I can smell burning fur and I start howling blue murder. Everyone in the restaurant glares at me, like I'm interrupting their dinner. *Me.* No one seems to be bothered by the tin-eared bastard ten feet away murdering 'Bat Out of Hell'. Eventually I have to go into the room and unplug the machine and inform the dickweed holding the mike that he might be a fat oaf but he's not Meat Loaf.

This gets me turfed out and I'm back on the street and it's good riddance as far as I'm concerned, because even though I specifically requested no MSG, those bastards laced the stuff with it and now I've got a headache that won't quit.

At the Crow Club, a members-only haunt that seems designed for big-game hunters, I'm ushered right through. The place is crammed six ways from Sunday. Pale half-moon faces, jostling elbows, industry louts and media pissheads, everyone trying to talk about everything at once, a furious imitation of parrots if parrots used the word *cunt* a lot.

The only seat I can find is at the bar.

'Nice to see you,' the barman says to me, overly familiar. 'What'll it be?'

'Just a shot of bourbon. Have I been in here before?'

'On many occasions.'

'Who am I?'

'You're Brian Blessed.'

'Right.'

'Aren't you?'

'Yes. Absolutely.'

He's off to mix up fruit-based concoctions. The table nearest me is full of hyperactive movie types celebrating some recent acquisition.

'We are going to defer this property and work the back end!' one of them shouts, a feverish man in too-wide pinstripes. One of his hands grips the table edge, the other a champagne bottle, as if he means to slam the whole thing into gear and drive them all to Hollywood.

'We are all going to reap scads!' he shrieks.

The others make a chorus of huzzahs, sounding like pirates. The table quakes. Perhaps the property in question *is* the table. It's apparent they're all coked to the gills. Looking around, I realise that *everyone in here is off their heads*. They drift off to the toilets furtively, then, moments later, come charging back out like white rhinos. Compared to this, my own transformation seems as mild as a heat rash.

I go back outside and stand on the pavement, trying to collate the vacant mystery of London nightlife into something I can fathom. I note the air of vomit. But I am in Soho and I have to accept the air of vomit. Then, from nowhere, paparazzi: a blinding frenzy of flash bulbs that turn night to day, and suddenly I'm down on my knees covering my face. I reach up and slap one of the cameras to the pavement and scream, 'Leave me alone, you ghoul!' at a photographer, and then I'm up on my feet again and running away, knifing through traffic. I look back only long enough to see that the paparazzi were not photographing me at all, but rather some actress who had emerged behind me, one of those current interchangeable tabloid waiflings named Kate or Cate or Caitlin or something or other.

I can see my big pointy nose in front of me and I set it for the end of the street and keep running, navigating the broken glass, the fist fights, the pavement pizzas, the shrieking legions of zombies, walking cadavers and hop-headed no-hopers. My sense of smell, entirely acute, absorbs this stifling miasma. Hops. Rain. Cocaine sweat. Bar varnish. Toilet cleaner. Hair gel. Congestion, dashed hopes, hallucinatory refrains: the internal moral collapse of a teeming city-state, its dire bowel chemistry.

My lungs feel like they're on fire.

Beneath a bank machine on Greek Street, I lie down beside a wino to catch my breath. The wino has intelligent features and seems resigned to his fate.

'You're a werewolf,' he says.

'Afraid so.'

'Are you going to mutilate me?'

'No. I'm going to be disappointed with you.'

'How can you be disappointed? You had no expectations of me. Might you be disappointed with society for letting me fall through the cracks?'

'That's how you think. I'm a werewolf. I treat everyone the same. If you were my friend I'd tell you to stop drinking and take control of your own life. Also bathe.'

'And as your friend I'd say I'm a sick-arse drunk and I can't do anything about it. Give us a quid.'

'I don't have any spare change.'

'I wouldn't take it from you anyway, you sanctimonious shite. I prefer spare change without the attendant life coaching.'

'Sorry,' I say and leave him and head down Oxford Street to catch a night bus.

I am a werewolf, but one with neither the resolve to murder or the balls to save someone from themselves. *I gotta stop drinking from hoofprints,* I say to myself, knowing full well that I won't. It's two a.m. The curse has worn off. My own pale skin is returning. My bones no longer feel translucent. I look around and see that I am just another night passenger, torn from his origins. Red and green lights shimmer on the riveted side of the bus, and beneath me my little suburban Chiswick shines, far away from Soho and the awful things that await it.

fort worth

IRBLE KELLER, FIVE years married, danced like a chicken on a hot plate while his wife called the tunes. That February, he drove from Amarillo to Fort Worth, Texas, filling up on low-test petrol so he could save enough money to buy a bottle of Early Times and celebrate getting away from her. He'd just taken a job as a special assistant to Chet Sampson, a man three years his junior.

'This is a job that can take you places,' Chet had said back in Amarillo, then added: 'Memorise everything.' Irble did, a range of subjects that ran from cattle futures to brand inspections, registries, breeding and veterinary records, various memorandums and driving distances. Amarillo to Fort Worth, for instance, was 386 miles.

'Check into the Double Tree Hotel on this voucher,' Chet had said, handing him a sheaf of info. 'Don't talk to anyone. You like steaks? Go to Mortons. Enjoy the Big City. Hit a titty bar, get shitfaced, what have you. But on Tuesday morning I need you in a state of absolute clarity. At ten a.m. two hundred thousand dollars will be wired directly into your checking account. You have until the closing bell to monitor the cattle futures. When instinct commands, call the number on the bottom of the page and make the buy. Immediately contact your bank and transfer the money. Whatever's left over stays in your account.'

It occurred to Irble that what he was being instructed to do wasn't entirely on the up and up, that in fact Chet was probably using a cattle buy to launder money. But Irble wasn't about to ask questions. At thirty-one, he saw himself on the precipice of success or failure. He planned to stay in Chet's employ only long enough to learn the livestock business, then shoot out on his own. There were specific things he wanted in life – solvency, for example – and Chet was offering him a chance at daylight. Yes, there was the question of $200,000 suddenly appearing on his bank statement. But it would be nothing more than a blip, a fat slab of bacon that would rest but briefly and leave behind a pleasant grease stain.

Irble's wife did not own a sense of humour, only a sense of ridicule. So when Irble informed her that Chet was sending him to Fort Worth 'on business' she said, quite risibly, 'Well I hope this amounts to something.' She was a cold-blooded miser at heart. Years ago she'd lost most of her money in a bunko scheme, and was determined not to have it happen again.

'Get yourself a pocket notebook and detail each expense,' she told him, then counted out just enough money to get him there and back. She demanded to know the name of the hotel he was staying in. Irble told her the Double Tree.

'Stay away from the room service,' she warned. 'They get you coming and going.'

92

Irble packed a small suitcase and looked around some-what wistfully at their house. He loved the little place and saw it as a monument to all he had to put up with from his wife.

He left the following morning. At the outskirts of Amarillo he turned on the radio, dialled in a big-kilowatt country station and hummed along:

> *Darling while you're busy burnin' bridges*
> *Burn one for me if you get time*

A fierce early-morning thunderstorm broke out. Irble squinted at the windshield like Mr Magoo and ploughed through the deluge. Most of the Plains were enduring a winter-long drought and the downpour only lasted a few minutes, but Irble enjoyed it for the feeling of putting a curtain between himself and his tortured home life.

Irble, who could instantly quote the opening and closing commodity numbers on Fort Worth steers, had never actually been to Fort Worth. His sister, Bryce, was there somewhere. They'd drifted apart years ago. On the drive down he'd thought about her, her striking wide mouth, her fixed froggy smile that anointed her with instant popularity all through their school years. It had always reminded Irble of the look on people's faces right before taking off on a roller coaster. They'd grown up together in a struggling part of Amarillo, raised by scrupulous, hardworking parents of Germanic descent. Bryce had lit out at sixteen. She seldom came back to visit, and when she did, Irble sensed in her something diminished, a gradual estrangement. Each subsequent visit, her famous smile seemed a bit more downturned, as if something in

Fort Worth was pulling her happiness into the ground. Now, seventeen years later, he had no idea how to find her.

When he got to Fort Worth, Irble checked into his hotel only to find the room unmade. He went back downstairs and reported this to the desk staffer, a small, ingratiating twenty-nothing who resembled a lizard in a suit. The lizard apologised absently, then disappeared behind a pair of swinging oak doors, making his exit as rude as possible. He returned moments later with a conciliatory offering: a dozen freshly baked oatmeal cookies. Irble wondered if there was a bakery in the hotel office. He wandered around the lobby idly munching the warm cookies and eyeing up the amenities. On the second-floor landing a number of business seminars were in progress. A sign outside one meeting room read: IS SATAN CUTTING INTO YOUR PROFITS?

Afterwards he returned to his room. It was still unchanged. He had a look around. The curtains and rumpled bedspread were done up in an explosive hibiscus pattern designed to make a tropical impression upon first entering the room. There was a minibar that was like a vision into the future. You could open it and see what a Dr Pepper was going to cost in the year 2020. For a long while he just stared in the mirror, examining himself in a context of new-found, if temporal, independence. He wore pressed jeans, a russet-colored snap-button shirt, polished cowboy boots and a belt buckle with a steer on it. The steer was well embedded into his generous paunch. He had raw-knuckled hands and a gleaming wedding band. He was not, by any stretch of the imagination, a lap-dance prospect. A ribeye was also out of the question. His wife would find out about that and throw a total conniption.

He left the hotel only once, to walk down the highway to a bank ATM where he extracted twenty dollars, then crossed the road to a package store for whisky and Doritos, a simple transaction that still seemed inescapable from his wife's wrath, as if he were hardwired to her vigilance. Sure enough, when he returned to his hotel room the phone message light was on. He picked it up and heard his wife's coarse voice. She wanted to know why he'd taken twenty dollars out of the bank.

He poured three fingers of whisky into a hotel glass and went to the window to sip it, gazing out at the sweep of Fort Worth, grey and caustic in the low winter light. The Trinity River was visible from where he stood, winding past the stockyards where congregations of cattle appeared as vaporous brown patches. Like them, Irble knew what it felt like to be hopelessly corralled.

He finished the whisky, poured himself another and finished that. Then he made two calls. The first was to Chet Sampson. He let the phone ring twenty times then hung up, fairly satisfied that Chet had already cleaned out his office and departed for some new climate of impunity. It was evident that Irble had been shunted to Fort Worth primarily to put time and distance between the two of them. That Chet had left him in the lurch both-ered him little.

Then he called his wife. She answered on the third ring.

'Do you know much a hotel call costs?' she yelped. 'I'll call you back.' She hung up.

Irble waited. The phone rang.

'What was the twenty dollars for?' his wife barked.

'Walking-around money,' he replied.

'Walking-around money? You're not like this. What's wrong?'

He thought he detected concern in her voice. He tried to find a caring comfort in this but it only made him worse off, more removed. He could picture exactly where she was standing, by the built-in desk in the corner of the dining room, next to the shelf with her collection of ballet figurines. He could picture these objects very clearly, as if they were personally forged for his memory. He could see their house, the single-bedroom railroader, plopped down in the frozen white void of north Amarillo, shabby but at least on the 'good' side of town, though you were never free of the wafting stench of the town's feedlots, its steaming vapours of offal and dismembered cattle parts cooking under the Texas sun. Beyond hamburger, Amarillo had nothing to offer the world.

'Nothing's wrong,' he said to his wife. 'It's nice to hear your voice.'

'Are you drunk?'

'A little . . .'

'In the middle of the day? You get laid off or something?'

'No.' He forced enthusiasm into his voice. 'In fact I sweetened that contract with that outfit I was telling you about the other day.'

He was trying to evince something: the impression of himself as his own man, a hard-working husband. He felt . . . he didn't know what he felt any more. He wanted to tell her that he was stifled by their life together but that maybe that was the true nature of love: the comfort of boredom.

'By the way . . .' he said, thumbing it in softly, 'tomorrow morning two hundred thousand dollars is going to pass through our checking account.'

'What does that mean, pass through?'

'It's only going to sit there for a few hours.'

'I don't understand . . .'

'Then it will be gone.'

'What do you mean . . . Who's . . . what two hundred thousand dollars?'

Suddenly, Irble was sick and tired of all of it. He had an urge to scream something vile at his wife, new words, totally uncharacteristic, things never uttered before. Instead he kept a steady voice.

'You know what? It's none of your goddamned business.'

There was a long pause on the line in which he imagined his wife being donkey-punched.

'What did you say?'

'I said I mean to take control of my own finances. I mean to pay off our mortgage. I mean to have walking-around money. And I mean to be no longer fiscally hounded by a harridan of a wife. Kiss my Yankee white ass.' He hung up and took a long slug of Early Times. He felt liberated.

Then Irble Keller, whose bank pin code was 9160 and whose mother's maiden name was Prosser, got drunk. Drunk at four in the afternoon. Drunk in a turbulently floral motel room in a nondescript Texas city, careening about, grinding Doritos from a half-eaten bag into the carpet with his bare feet, cradling a fresh bottle of Early Times while the bedside radio blared cattle market futures. At some point there was a knock on the door, the sound of a passkey, and a maid entered pushing a Rubbermaid trolley. She was a compact Latino with a look of weary bereavement. Irble waved, overly friendly, and she smiled back. He tottered at the edge of the bed, watching her clear the sheets. A vague notion began to stir in him that she might actually want to sleep with him. He felt gloriously winsome and self-owned and he cranked up the gee-howdy Texan act to an almost farcical level.

'You ever hear a drawl like mine?' he said to her.

She ignored him. She spoke perfect English and to her most Texans sounded the same: like they launched their sentences from a cannon. She went into the bathroom, partially closed the door behind her, took a can of industrial cleaner off the trolley and started in on the tub.

Irble appeared, pushing the door open with his foot, leaning unsteadily against the bathroom door.

'You're playin' this to the hilt, aren't you?' he slurred. It had been a long time since he'd been this rat-assed.

'I'm from Amarillo,' he boomed. 'Cattle business. This is flying in the face of my instincts but, hey, I don't get to the big city that much. Yessiree . . . you are something else!' He exuded a lusty, appreciative whistle, then waddled back into the bedroom momentarily, returned dangling the Early Times in one hand, rubbing at his crotch with the other, steadfast in his examination of her. When he set the bottle on the sink ledge and clumsily tried to paw her breasts, she grabbed it by the neck and cracked it over his head.

The impact of this on Irble was a jarring epiphany, not entirely sexual. For a fraction of a second he seemed to see a white space in his life, an echo of something his imagination had only trifled with. His life had become sonorous with the dread of debt and failure. Being smacked in the head with a whisky bottle was a real wake-me-up, possibly emasculating, certainly invigorating.

'That's exactly what I needed,' he said. A warm rivulet of blood snaked down his brow. It probably didn't occur to him how depraved he appeared to the maid.

'Try that again, I go for the police,' she said, trying to sidestep him.

'Hit me again,' he said.

'I got six more rooms to get through,' she said. She handed the bottle back to him, then skirted past toward the bedroom door, using the trolley as a buffer. He slumped down on the bed and gurgled a slug of whisky.

'Am I ever the horse's ass,' he muttered as she slammed the door behind her. He listened as the trolley squeaked across the hallway carpet. There was a perfunctory knock on the next door, and he hoped the incident was gone from his life. He suddenly felt light-headed. Soon enough he would discover that this was because the whisky bottle had dislodged several pieces of vital information from his memory.

Twenty minutes later there was a knock on the door. Irble imagined the police. For some reason it seemed important to put his shoes on. The passkey made a click and the maid walked in. He stood frozen at her approach, cowboy boot in hand, extended as if to keep her at bay.

She handed him a glossy postcard.

'I found this under the bed a few rooms up. Looks like it's right up your alley.'

Irble took the card.

She aimed her gaze directly at the welt she had administered to his head.

'Sometimes,' she said, 'I have to pluck stray pubes out of the bathtub. Or clear a bedsheet covered in someone's period blood. Neither of those activities disgusts me as much as you.'

When she'd left, Irble looked at the card. It was an advertisement: a blonde girl in a lurid, coercive pose. HOT SLUT MAID WILL VISIT YOUR HOME OR HOTEL, the print said. Had he been a bit keener, sober perhaps, the irony of this would have settled on him.

Irble sat down on the bed and studied the blonde in the ad: hair upswept, stuffed into a shiny chequered corset that struck Irble as ill suited for manoeuvring into those stubborn hard-to-clean areas. But the disconcerting part was the woman's face. It didn't look slutty. It looked open and friendly, the kind of face only profound innocence could produce. And the roller-coaster smile was unmistakable. The face belonged to his sister, Bryce.

He sat for a long, long time. There was the distinct feeling that things were unravelling here in Fort Worth. For some reason his earliest recollection of Bryce and himself came to mind. Their parents had taken them horseback riding: someone's ranch or farm, that part he wasn't clear on. But he remembered the sheer enormity of the animal, a big roan mare with flared nostrils who stamped impatiently at the dirt, haltered in place by its owner.

'Rein her tight or she'll take both of you into the next world,' the owner had said. Irble remembered those words exactly, even if at the time – he couldn't have been more than four – he didn't quite know what the owner meant. Suddenly, with a boost from his father, Irble was astride. The owner handed him the reins, slapped the horse's flank and Irble had floated out of the corral, feeling the huge rolling gait of the animal beneath him. He had never experienced such majesty. His sister, on the other hand, never got on the horse. She was terrified of the animal and ran off in hysterics.

There was a phone number on the postcard. He went around the bed, picked up the phone and dialled the number. His chest felt constricted. A deep voice, a man's voice, answered.

'Yeah.'

'I'm calling about the maid.' His own voice, nervous and reedy, lacked essential Texas bombast.

'Which maid?'

'The blonde one. The one on the card.'

'We got three, fo' blondes here. Take your pick.'

'Her name is Bryce.'

'Bryce. No one here answers to that name.'

'She'll answer to me. I'm her brother.'

'Said what?'

Irble made an effort to correct his voice.

'My name is Irble Keller. I would like to speak to my sister.'

There was a long pause.

'Where you at?'

'The Double Tree Hotel.'

'Double Tree. Un hunh. What room.'

Irble couldn't remember. This was slightly worrying. He never forgot numbers.

'Hang on a sec.' He set the receiver on the bed, went to the door and came back.

'Room 3124,' he said.

'Said the Double Tree?'

'Yeah.'

'See what I can do.' The voice hung up. Irble's insides pinwheeled. He quaffed the last of the Early Times, suffered a panic of disassociation, flitted through the radio channels until he found something familiar on a Country Classics station. He sat on his bed, slightly concussed, very drunk, but fully aware that some dangerously simple bravery had alighted in him. How durable it would become he had no idea. Eventually there was a meaty thump on the door. Irble went to open it. A black man filled the doorway, dreadlocked, easily six foot six. He wore a thick leather trench coat that brought to mind

101

seventies blaxploitation figures. He gave Irble a clinical once-over.

'You bleedin' from the head,' he said.

'Where's Bryce?'

'First things first,' the big man replied, walking Irble back into the room. He gave off a strong odour, like charity shop camphor. He crossed the room and stood at the window. 'The main thing about me is I'm orderly and professional. Act like a gentleman and we gonna get through this like gangbusters.' He looked out the window, then back at Irble.

'Who are you?' said Irble.

'I'm the guy who sees after the girls,' he answered. 'That's in between bench pressing three-fifty. You wanna see her?'

'I do.'

'That's good, 'cause she wants to see you.'

'All right.'

'But first I need two hundred dollars.'

'That's crazy.'

'Say that again?'

'I'm not paying you a goddamn cent.'

'Come over to the window,' he said. 'Show you something.' Irble went to the window. The pimp indicated a blue Chevy Suburban idling in the motel parking lot.

'See the blue rig?' he said.

Irble recognised his sister sitting in the back seat, nervously tapping a cigarette out the window.

'That's Lemon Drop,' the pimp said. 'Lemon Drop's got a full dance card tonight. You wanna see her, tick tock . . . the clock's runnin'.'

'Lemon Drop?'

'Her workin' name.'

'Her name is Bryce.'

'Pay up. She'll be whoever you want her to be.' He gave a thin reptilian smile, and added, 'Bro.'

Irble eyed the empty whisky bottle on the bed, calculated going for it. Unlike the Mexican maid's cautionary tap, he would have to swing for the upper decks to put this lummox down. The pimp seemed to read his mind and wagged a big finger at him.

'Reconsider,' he said, flatly.

Irble absorbed this as part of his trajectory of declining hope. He sat down on the bed and put his head in his hands.

'This isn't winding out the way I imagined it.'

'You a real droll guy, aren't ya? Two hundred or I fix your little red wagon.'

'Listen,' said Irble. 'I'm in way over my head. I don't wanna get involved in sleaze. I just want to see my sister.'

'By association that's implies I'm sleazy.'

'No. I didn't mean that. I'm sure you're just a regular guy.'

'I'm a pimp. I get money. You get your happy ending. That's the way it's worked since biblical times.'

'I don't have any money.'

'Credit card?'

Irble sighed, then pulled out his wallet and let his lone credit card drop from a plastic accordion.

'Take it. You can keep it. Forge my signature. Whatever you want. I don't know how this works.'

'How what works?' the pimp said.

'How anything works any more.'

'Real simple,' said the pimp and reached into his coat pocket. He pulled out a small black console for accepting credit cards. Irble would have been hardly less joyed if it had been a gun, which could only relieve you of cash in hand. This thing could cut all the way down to your bank's daily interest payments. The pimp held it forward and Irble, with a doomed sense of duty, slid his card in. There followed a series of bleeps in which Irble imagined his financial history being compressed, and then the screen asked for his pin number. Irble froze up.

'Wha's wrong?' said the pimp.

'My pin number. It's slipped my mind.'

The pimp yanked out the credit card, placed the console back in his pocket, and went to the window, staring out with what looked like an all-purpose disgust for this particular line of work.

'Life used to be so simple,' he said deflatedly. 'Now we got to do things the hard way.' Irble steeled himself, fully expecting to be punched, welcoming it in fact. If one blow had knocked his pin number out of him, he reasoned, another might return it. Instead, the pimp pulled out a mobile phone and pushed a lone digit. Irble sat and listened while the pimp iterated his card details to some unseen figure, directing two hundred dollars of Irble's money toward Hot Slut Maids Incorporated. Irble jumped to his feet.

'Whoa, whoa, whoa!' he yelled.

'Hold on,' said the pimp and covered the mouthpiece. 'What?'

'Hot Slut Maids Incorporated?'

'That's the name of the business.'

'That's how it shows up on my statement? Hot Slut Maids?

The pimp looked confounded.

'Couldn't you have named it something less obvious?' said Irble.

'I don't make those kind of executive decisions. I'm more in the enforcement side of things. Besides,' he added, 'you shoulda thought of that before you ordered the girl.'

Irble was envisioning his wife now, who often sat at the dining room desk monitoring their online bank statements like a hawkish air traffic controller. Well, this one was going to be a real doozy. Whatever vengeful glee that thought gave him was tempered by the knowledge that he could never, ever go home again.

The pimp finished the transaction and hung up.

'Done and done,' he announced. 'I'll send her up now.' He brushed past Irble. Before he could reach the door, the room phone rang. No doubt Hot Slut Maids had just crash-landed.

'If it's all the same to you,' said Irble, 'I'll see her in your car.'

The first thing his sister did when he climbed in the back seat of the Suburban was to give him a precarious hug. For a while, neither of them spoke. It was enough to just sit there quietly and absorb the languorous, slightly heartbroken reunion. Irble kept sneaking glances at her. She didn't much resemble the cake-decorated, airbrushed Bryce in the ad. There were terrible bags under her eyes that made it seem as if she could see far beyond the present situation. Still, he thought, it would be a strange individual who didn't find his sister lovely.

'Well . . .' she finally said. 'This isn't how I would have planned a get-together.'

'Amen to that,' Irble said.

'What have you gotten up to?' she asked. 'Still in Amarillo?'

'I'm running away from the wife.'

'Why?'

'She doles out joy in an eyedropper, that's why.'

'Not much different than me,' she said, and indicated the pimp, who at that moment was in the parking lot, executing forearm curls with a dumbbell. 'Welcome to the jungle.'

She saw the blood on his head and extracted some baby wipes from an oversized red bag.

'He do that to you?' she asked.

'No. It was a maid.'

'A maid?'

'A hotel maid. I had this plan to reform her, teach her English then run off together to Cozumel.' The lanolin smell of the baby wipe took him back to some comforting moment of infancy until it occurred to him that she probably used them to wipe up jizz. Abruptly, Irble asked his sister if she was a drug addict.

She started a soft lilt. '*I'm on the drugs. I'm off the drugs. I'm on the drugs. I'm off the drugs. I'm on the drugs. I'm off the drugs. Sometimes I even sell the drugs . . .* little song I'm working on . . .' She laughed, dabbing at his temple. The frog smile appeared. For a moment Irble felt supremely exhilarated. His sister's presence had the effect of a light at the bottom of a deep freeze. They both went silent again and Irble used this interlude to test his numerical memory. He noted the number on the licence plate of a parked car – YT567 – then looked away. The number vanished from his mind, just like that

'I was thinkin' about that time they took us horseback riding,' he said. 'You remember?'

'Yeah. What brought that on?'

'You were terrified. I was thinkin' . . .'

'What?'

'Well, I was thinkin' had you climbed on that horse, things might've turned out different.'

'Different in what way?'

'Maybe you would have understood the truly fragile

control someone has over a beast, any kind of beast, that can take them into another world.'

'That's an astonishing statement, Irble,' she said. 'Very astute of you to point out the exact moment you think my life took a nosedive. You don't know me and you never will.'

This rebuke made Irble realise he was no longer etherised. Reality was emerging in the form of a crippling hangover that seemed to be gathering at his eyeballs. For a second, the mundane comforts of his home and marriage came to mind. He thought of the smell of his wife's cold cream, lying open in a jar beside the bedroom sink, the calendar on the kitchen wall that always seemed unturned and two months behind. Without familiarity you're truly alone, he thought, and felt a simple but painful ache in his heart for his lost sister.

'I'm taking you away from here,' he announced.

'I knew it,' she said, and with an extended finger whirred the electric window down.

'Here comes the rescue attempt!' she called to the pimp. 'What'd I tell you?' The pimp stopped mid-curl and glared in Irble's direction. Irble noted that the veins in his arm were roughly the diameter of a common garden hose. She rolled the window back up.

'That wasn't funny,' he said.

'You sound determined to leave Fort Worth with a damsel under your arm. But to tell you the truth, I like it here just fine.'

'What kind of life you call this?'

'You never had a prostitute?'

'No. Of course not.'

'It's not a disgrace. I try to see what I do as a gift that perpetuates joy to lonely individuals.'

'You're a whore.'

'When did you get so cynical? My needs are catered for. You paid him two hundred? I get to keep sixty.'

Irble fumbled with these numbers but came up blank. He found it deeply depressing that he couldn't even calculate the percentage at which his sister was being exploited.

'How's Mom and Dad?' she asked.

'Gone.'

'Both of them?'

'Yeah.'

'When?'

Once again he panicked. Exact years and dates had evaporated from his mind. *When was it? Three years ago? Five?* Irble needed numbers because it was numbers that would shape his future. But they'd all flitted away.

'I don't remember, Bryce. I'm blanking all of a sudden.'

He related the story of their deaths to her as if it were pure reportage, removed from his own experience.

'Maybe a year apart from each other. The Old Man went first. He had a stroke . . . at his computer. He had this project: puttin' together the family tree, something. He just keeled over. Mom told everyone at the service she found him facedown on the keyboard, lifted his head and typed his name on to a branch. Her little joke. Anyway, a year or so later she caught pneumonia. That led to lots of other complications that they cleared up. But in the end they never got the pneumonia.'

'I'm sorry to hear that, Irble,' she said, as if talking about someone very distant. They seemed to sense each other's detachment from what should have been tragic information. Then she asked Irble an astonishing question:

'Has it occurred to you we were adopted?'

He sat stunned. She watched him complacently, letting the idea sink in.

'Believe me,' she said, 'this isn't the first crazy notion

I've floated, but it never seems to go away. Why else would we feel so disconnected?'

Irble could only conclude that this was some drama she had cooked up in one of her pharmacological fogs, something to do with shifting blame perhaps, and told her so.

'Is that what you think?' she seethed. 'When you've been in and out of as many programmes as me, Irble, you'll come to understand what the word *care* means. And I'm telling you, those two never knew what to do with us. They were well-meaning Lutherans who did what well-meaning Lutherans do. They looked after us. But I'm not so fucked up I can't distinguish between love and obligation.'

She lit a cigarette and sent a furious plume out into the evening air.

'I'm sure we were adopted,' she said again and crossed her arms with a kind of finality.

Irble went quiet and stared out the window at Fort Worth spreading out in every direction, all hard angles and flat low buildings, mesquite and concrete: the West grudgingly giving way to something frightening and alien. He observed a flattened armadillo, like a hardened bedroom slipper, lying not ten feet from the car. There and then a flood of something akin to aloneness passed from his sister to him, filling up the vacuum that had occupied so much of his life.

'Then it follows,' he reasoned, 'that quite possibly you and I aren't really related.'

'That doesn't mean you get to fuck me,' she answered, and Irble genuinely couldn't tell if this was a joke or not.

The pimp came over and rapped on the window, then pointed to his watch, indicating Irble's time was up. Irble brought the window down and motioned for the pimp to lean in.

'Let me ask you a question,' he said.

'Fire away.'

He indicated Bryce. 'Her and me. You see any resemblance?'

The pimp didn't really take his eyes off Irble.

'I do,' he answered. 'But then again, ya'll look the same to me. Get outta my car.'

Irble kissed his sister goodbye and watched the Suburban drive out of the parking lot and speed away. In the end, he chalked it up as a rather extraordinary day. He went up to his room and stood at the window, watching the moon strain upward in a sky lashed with purple. The lights of Fort Worth sparkled. He couldn't understand why, in such an unknown place, he still felt some kind of desperate freedom. Free to order room service. Free to run off with a stranger. Free of the past.

He lay down on the bed and drifted into a kind of demented half-sleep while the radio played. A fire-and-brimstone preacher was shouting in a hyperactive hog-caller voice that the current drought was undeniable proof that Jesus was furious with all of us: that the attendant high pollen count was Him adding insult to injury. Later, the programme switched to country music. As Irble slept fitfully, the numbers 0 through 9 appeared in his head, decked out in Western regalia, performing a line dance: more or less the Electric Slide. Eventually four of the numbers stepped forward, arranged themselves into his pin code and doffed their hats.

When Irble awoke Tuesday morning, he tuned the radio to the cattle futures, then went into the bathroom. By the time he came out, the price had dropped four cents to seventy-nine per hundredweight. All over Texas, young underfed cattle were being brought into feedlots: a hedge against the foreseeable long-scale plains drought. Apparently Jesus *was* mad, because in the next hour the futures dropped a further three increments. The market threatened to close early for a recoup, so Irble picked up the phone and dialled the number Chet had given him.

He put in a market buy order for the units Chet had specified. The broker on the other end wanted to know who to charge the order to. As a joke, Irble told him the buyer was doing business as Hot Slut Maids Incorporated, then gave Chet Sampson's last known address. The broker accepted this humourlessly and didn't even ask for the spelling. Irble's margin came out at $121,000.

Then Irble called his bank in Amarillo. He cycled through a litany of digital voices until he reached a human. He told the voice he wished to wire-transfer $121,000 to the Fort Worth Commodities Exchange.

'Account number?' the voice said.

Irble reeled it off without a beat.

'Sort code?'

'23-76-78,' said Irble.

There would be enough left over to pay off his mortgage and start a handsome new life elsewhere. He was thinking maybe Mexico.

'Mother's maiden name?' said the voice.

'Well now,' said Irble. 'That's an interesting question.'

golf sale

Here he comes . . . the Potential Customer . . .
churning up the pavement with his nose in his
mobile phone, dialling up his next heart attack.
He's got eight million things to do and they were
all due yesterday. A chipping wedge and a twelve-pack
of Titleists are the last things on his mind. Till he
looks up and see me. Suddenly, for a moment, for
just a moment . . . the pavement melts away. He's
transported to a land of green and pastoral velvet,
a Fairway to Heaven.

Golf Sale.

Beneath those two words an arrow, emphatic
and immutable, pointing down an alley. And the
soul processes what the overprogrammed brain
can't. Because the soul longs for escape from the
tyranny of the workday. The soul knows that the last
true drama left on this planet isn't the sub-prime

mortgage rate or the NASDAQ index, it's one's handicap. And the soul follows that arrow.

Golf Sale

You like numbers? Chew on these. Last year the world spent £422 million on club sets. It purchased 11.6 million units of individual clubs, 211.3 million dozen golf balls, 11.3 million pairs of shoes. Golf equipment sales have increased by an average of 2.7% annually for the last ten years running . . . in fact golf equipment outsells all other sports equipment combined. In so many words, selling golf equipment is a licence to print money. That's why so many passers-by pretend to act like we don't exist. They're resentful because we're the hub of a blue-chip industry, and maybe, just maybe, they can't handle that fact.

From *Reginald Dawson's Highly Successful Secrets to Standing on a Corner Holding Up a Golf Sale Sign*

As you read my now-classic book, *Reginald Dawson's Highly Successful Secrets to Standing on a Corner Holding Up a Golf Sale Sign*, you'll probably find yourself nodding your head and saying, 'Finally! Some useful advice on how to persuade busy pedestrians to impulsively turn down a wino-piss-puddled alleyway into a musty warehouse to plop down five hundred quid for a new set of titanium clubs even though they've never played a round of golf in their life!'

That's why my book is a rarity: a 'secrets' book that actually provides you with useful tactics that you can employ on any corner anywhere in the world. In fact, the knowledge you gain from this book will come in just as handy in *everyday life situations* as it does in the survival of your own business.

WHO AM I?

I'm Reginald Dawson, that's who: the world's most successful Human Directional. (Yep, that's the professional term for People Who Stand on Corners All Day Holding Up Signs.)

Get this straight. Standing on a corner holding a sign is *what I do*. It's what I'm about. When I'm not standing on a corner holding a *Golf Sale* sign, I'm *thinking* about standing on a corner holding a *Golf Sale* sign. My no-nonsense style will show you how you can be a successful Human Directional without lowering yourself to the sleazy gimmicks many Human Directionals resort to.

People would normally pay a lot of money for the secrets revealed in my book, *Reginald Dawson's Highly Successful Secrets to Standing on a Corner Holding Up a Golf Sale Sign*. Naturally, you're wondering if my claims are truly valid or if I'm just a fly-by-night popinjay peddling yet another book that claims to divulge the inner secrets of successful Golf Sale signholding. Well, read the tips below. Incorporate them into your own sign-holding approach and see if your traffic doesn't increase immediately!

TIP 1: LET 'EM TALK! LET 'EM WALK!

Remember, 99.99% of the traffic coming toward you will give you a dismissive, even hostile look and continue on. Congratulations! You've been noticed! And *Getting Noticed* is *exactly halfway* to *Closing the Sale*. Occasionally, you'll even overhear a choice comment directed your way: 'Why does that fuckwit stand in the same goddamn spot day in and day out holding up a stupid sign?' for example. That, my friend, is called *Establishing a Relationship*. It's crucial in *Closing the*

Sale to make your Potential Customer think *he's* controlling the transaction. He needs to feel superior. So just let him walk on by. *Make him think he's winning!*

TIP 2: EMPATHISE, DON'T PATRONISE

The brutal truth is, most of the human traffic approaching you has a complete and abject indifference to discount golf equipment. You need to empathise with this attitude by putting yourself in the Potential Customer's shoes and showing *that same indifference*. Nothing is more powerful than being in sync with the mindset of the customer. It shows you're on their side and you want to work with them.

By all means avoid smiling or eye contact of any kind. Smiling sends the wrong message. It says, 'I understand you're suffering from a severe lack of golfing accessories.' That's patronising. People from every walk of life are coming your way – Somalians, teenage ghetto rappers, women, etc. – it's possible some of them have never even *heard* of the sport of golf, so don't condescend to them by smiling and pretending you understand their plight. Be authentic.

TIP 3: YOU WANT THIS JOB BUT YOU DON'T <u>NEED</u> THIS JOB

A calculated lack of interest in your work is vital to success. It's my experience that if you *need* to sell discount golf equipment you probably won't. You'll look too tense, too desperate, too eager. Remember, your body language is critical because Potential Customers believe what they *see* more than what they *read*. Let your Potential Customer see you drinking Tennants from a litre can while idly working on a Sudoku. This makes the Potential Customer think, 'He acts like he doesn't even *want* me to know about the Golf Sale . . . like I'm some two-bit loser who's unentitled to discount golf equipment. Well, goddammit, I'm *somebody* and I'm going down that alley.' Next thing you know, he'll have plopped down five large on a new set of titanium Wilsons. *People want what they can't have.*

Sometimes I'll even let the *Golf Sale* sign drift off a few degrees so it actually points in the wrong direction. Again, this is purely calculated. Once your Potential Customer has wandered down the wrong street and invested a little shoe leather, he's gonna be a lot more determined to find the Golf Sale and reward his efforts.

TIP 4: NEVER ADMIT RIGHT AWAY THAT THERE IS A GOLF SALE

Occasionally, a Potential Customer may actually approach you with an enquiry about the Golf Sale. They may, for example, want to know what brand names are on sale, or what kind of markdown is being offered. Regard them quizzically and ask, 'What Golf Sale?' Explain you're just holding the sign for a friend. Or tell them you're actually *protesting* against Golf Sales. Whatever you do, deny the existence of the Golf Sale. Psychology supports this gambit. Acknowledging that there *is* a Golf Sale triggers one of two responses in your Potential Customer: 'Something must be wrong' or 'I could probably do better somewhere else.' You don't want to plant that kind of negativity in your Potential Customer's head. Trust me, the more you deny the existence of a Golf Sale, the more they'll be convinced there *is* one, and it must be pretty goddamn special if you're being so evasive about it.

At this point a savvy Potential Customer may try to

deploy what we in the business call the *Vice Technique*. The Vice Technique is when the Potential Customer sees through your *Denial Ploy* and tries to squeeze the truth out of you. In so many words he is trying to negotiate a concession. He may say, for instance, 'Oh, you have to do better than that.' Or quite possibly something a little more salient, like 'Are you out of your fucking mind?' If this technique is used on you, keep your negotiating margin tight. Counter with 'How much better do I have to do?' or 'How far out of my fucking mind do you need me to be?' This response puts the ball back in his court.

TIP 5: STAY ON YOUR CORNER

Not to rub your face in it, but I pull down thirty large a day. (And by *large*, I mean pounds.) And here's the kicker. *I don't even know the name of the place I'm advertising!* (I think it's Manny's World of Golf. Or maybe Manny's Golf World.) At the close of each business day, one of Manny's assistants will come up to the corner and discreetly hand me a rolled-up wad of cash. Not only is this *making the company come to me* (see my chapter on *Self-Empowerment*), but it also keeps me from having to walk down the alley and enter Manny's premises. Because when I'm in Manny's, I'm distracted. I'm looking around at inventory. I'm looking at lighting, product rotation, point of purchase displays, shipping rotations, etc. In other words, I'm *Off My Corner.* I'm imagining what I would do if I was in charge of these particular aspects of the business, and this is *Misdirected Focus.*

Stay on your corner. You're a motivated person. It's perfectly natural to want to do everything. Remind yourself that there are underlings who are responsible for all that stuff. *Your job is to stand on the corner and hold up a Golf Sale sign.*

TIP 6: DRIVE APPROPRIATELY TOWARD CLOSING THE DEAL

Once you've got the Potential Customer looking at your sign (see my chapter on *Taking the Bait*), subtly turn the sign as they pass by to keep it in their periphery. This indicates you are 'willing to bend' and committed to serving their needs.

You may, on occasion, recognise a person because they pass by at the same time each day. It's a common mistake to assume these people must work nearby. Never dismiss them as Potential Customers. After all, if they really weren't interested in what you had to offer *they'd have changed their route.* They are indicating a gradual willingness to pursue discount golf equipment. In a sense they are moving toward a decision. Be patient and maintain a can-do attitude.

I'm Reginald Dawson and I'm giving you these tips absolutely free because *I know you'll want to come back for more.* Don't think of *Reginald Dawson's Highly Successful Secrets to Standing on a Corner Holding Up a Golf Sale Sign* as a book. Think of *Reginald Dawson's Highly Successful Secrets to Standing on a Corner Holding Up a Golf Sale Sign* as a tool. A tool that will not only provide you with profound and accessible strategies for turning your God-given sign-holding talent into instant cash but will actually inspire you at every hole in this game we call Life. Buy now with money-back confidence.

prairie dogs

IN APPEARANCE, THE prairie dog falls somewhere between the meerkat and the squirrel. It uses its hind legs ferociously, like a jackhammer, to construct a system of tunnels that can eventually ruin someone's ranch.

Once entrenched, it's a real bastard to remove.

Since they'd moved to this house, this country place, Dave Slocum had tried to feel some commonality with his neighbours, in particular the men with their big weathered faces and bruised knuckles who made their living with their hands. Now, having decided to plant winter wheat, he was starting to feel a part of their stock. He had spent two days tilling his sixty acres, three perfect twenty-acre sections defined by sagging four-rail fencing. He had a pitiable little Farmall tractor: certainly nothing like those John Deere juggernauts the old-timers around here owned, or rather *the bank* owned: Dave knew that these days the primary ranch skill wasn't planting or irrigating or harvesting, but making the monthly nut on behemoth equipment. Thus he had no interest in full-time ranching. He and his new wife, Marcie, had moved to this part of Montana three months ago. Newly married is like being described the daytime and not the night. Thus they were both giddy with optimism. Dave invested everything he had in a golf course over in Ennis. But the course stayed frozen for five months of the year so Dave had decided to give winter farming a shot. His plan, come springtime, was to sell the grain to the biofuel plant over in Three Forks. Maybe then there would be some money to fix up their new house.

He stood at the crest of a small hill and admired his tractorwork. The old Farmall sat idle beside him, heat coming off the engine. It was early September and there was a crazy hot light over everything, magnified by the tight yellow furrows he'd just made in his land. Beyond his fields the valley made an abbreviated rise toward the Tobacco Root Mountains, which looked black and forged and, as mountains go, somewhat unfinished. He was still new enough to this place to have that kind of vista overwhelm him.

He watched with idle fascination as a buteo hawk drifted down from a coulee, circled gracefully three times, then plucked up a prairie dog by the nape of its neck. The prairie dog sailed away. For some reason this reminded Dave of his honeymoon. He and Marcie had taken a cruise out of Miami on the Royal Caribbean Line. Their first night they had gone to see a comedian in the showroom. The comedian was way out of his element, and when his material got nothing but confused stares from the crowd, he turned belligerent. Marcie and Dave, who had never seen a live stand-up before, sat there watching him implode until he was nothing more than protoplasm and flop sweat. The crowd, primarily retirees and newlyweds, wasn't remotely sympathetic to his plight, and being collectively referred to as fish-faced cunts certainly wasn't part of the all-inclusive fun package they'd been promised. Afterwards everyone stood out on the deck and watched the comedian being helicoptered away at the end of a rope.

The prairie dog, dangling helplessly in the hawk's grip, made Dave think of this.

He left the tractor where it sat and came back over the rise toward his house. It was nothing to write home about, the house, but then why would you need to? It *was* home: a yellow clapboarded single-storey with modest windows, built for looking out of, not into.

Dave noticed an ungainly vehicle parked on the lawn. He couldn't quite grasp it at first. It seemed to be an old flatbed Ford truck with a huge Plexiglas chamber attached to the back.

What's going on here? he thought to himself as he got closer. A portable corncrib, perhaps? Some kind of incubator? Directly behind the truck's cab was a compression device, a protrusion of frayed wires and corroded valves that connected to an expanding coil slathered in duct tape. At the end of the coil was a nozzle the size of a howitzer cannon. From stem to stern, the monstrosity oozed oil and joint grease. Indeed, a purplish viscous puddle had collected underneath the crankcase, fouling Dave's yard. It was a Frankenstein contraption, ridiculously home-made. Dave imagined its owner being laughed out of every patent attorney's office in the land. What he didn't imagine was that the owner, who possessed a reduced view of humankind, would not have stood for that kind of ridicule for a second. The vehicle belonged to Tellis Wondersweet. Around this part of

Montana, Tellis Wondersweet was known as the Prairie
Dog Man, and at this very moment he was inside Dave's
kitchen, leering at his wife.

'This is the man who left his card in our mailbox,' said
Marcie.

'How ya doing?' said Dave.

'Oh . . .' replied Tellis, pausing in that way some people
do to put a black cloud around an innocuous greeting,
'fair to middlin'.' He had a mean but not unhandsome
face, dark and lined like a walnut. Cockiness radiated
from him, a kind of swagger that made Dave Slocum
uneasy. He was slouched at the table beside Marcie, a
little too close for Dave's liking. His underslung cowboy
boots jutted on to the floor, scuffing the linoleum.

Marcie said, 'I was just telling Mr Wondersweet—'

'Tellis.'

'Tellis . . . about the prairie dog I hit on the road the
other day. Right out there.' She indicated the highway
running by their house. 'He ran out before I could do a
thing about it. I mean, I was gutted.'

'My wife is British,' Dave explained. 'Brits can't stand
to see an animal in misery because Brits desire all misery
for themselves.'

Tellis seemed to wait just a second too long to get that
this was a joke.

'I stopped the car and got out to see if he was still
alive,' Marcie said. 'And then another one ran out and
tried to drag him to safety.'

Tellis Wondersweet decided it unnecessary to tell her
the prairie dog was actually dragging its buddy away to
eat it.

'It's just a prairie dog, babe,' Dave said. He measured
the distance Tellis was sitting from his wife, then sat down

and equalled it. They all seemed unnaturally huddled for such a large table.

Marcie fixed him with a stare. 'Well, suffering does not make nature a better place.'

'She's got a point there, Dave,' Tellis said, taking yet another wildly conspicuous survey of her cleavage.

'That's quite a rig you got parked out there, Mr Wondersweet,' Dave said. 'What exactly does it do?'

'Sucks up prairie dogs.'

'Come again?'

'You heard me. The EPA's been tryin' to shut me down for years. But they can't do jackshit. 'Cause I'm perfectly within my rights.'

He launched into a practised description of prairie dog activity.

'Unabated, the prairie dog will dig a series of tunnels that eventually collapses the ground, causing livestock to break their legs.'

'We don't own livestock,' Dave said.

'And he'll go after your crops.'

Marcie looked worried. Dave noted the black half-moons of grease under the man's fingernails and wanted him and his ugly contraption off their property.

'Now you tell me,' Tellis went on, 'what's more humane? To suck them up with a modified grain vacuum where they are nothing more than momentarily stunned, or to eviscerate them with a .22?'

Marcie visibly blanched at this. It was fairly obvious that Tellis was pulling her strings.

They'd run into this problem before. One time Dave had come home with a bug zapper, a tennis-racquet-shaped thing that gave off a crisp and satisfying report every time it made contact with a flying insect. He started waving it around the kitchen light, sizzling everything in sight, and the room quickly filled up with a smell like burnt almonds. Marcie went nuts.

'You want bugs?' Dave said.

'No. But look at you. You're demonic.'

'Damned right I am. Wanna go at it?' He handed her the zapper. She dashed it on the edge of the kitchen counter.

Tellis Wondersweet described an overtly graphic picture of a prairie dog being assassinated.

'Now if you plug one with your normal .22 they'll just perform a furry, cinematic little death dance and keel over. But around these parts, folks are partial to the steel-tipped cartridge.' Here he cannily looked Marcie straight in the eye. 'The steel-tip does to a prairie dog roughly what a nine-iron does to a toadstool.' He turned to Dave. 'Your wife tells me you're a golfer.'

'I own a golf course,' Dave corrected him.

'Don't play myself. Never saw the sense of knocking a little white ball all over God's creation. Anyway, what do you reckon?'

'About what?'

'You want me to hoover up your prairie dogs?'

'How much will it cost?'

'Two hundred dollars. You get my guarantee with that.'

Dave absorbed this like a gut punch, as if their meagre bank account was actually lodged in his stomach.

'What do you do with them once they're caught?' Marcie asked.

'Sell them to an overseas exporter. The Japs use them for pets.'

This wasn't remotely the case. All Tellis did, when the big Plexiglas cage was full, was drive them across the river and let them go. Then he would wait a week or so and start working that side of the river. In this way, his career, if you could call it that, perpetuated itself.

'Let us think about it,' said Marcie.

When Tellis was driving away Dave said, 'Doesn't he even have the sense to put side-view mirrors on that thing? It's a death machine.'

'I don't believe he's as dumb as you think.'

'I don't want that truck around here. I'm going to borrow a .22 and get rid of those prairie dogs myself.'

'You most certainly are not.'

And that, effectively, was the first nail being hammered into Dave Slocum's marriage.

Tellis showed up two days later. He combed the top pasture while Dave walked alongside opening the gates. The flatbed sputtered and rattled, spewing an acrid black cloud from its strangled exhaust. You will recall that a flatbed Ford is mentioned in the Eagles' song 'Take It Easy'. In that song a girl, my lord, in a flatbed Ford slows down to take a look at the lead singer. No such girl occupied Tellis's rig. Instead it slowly filled up with prairie dogs and they only looked baffled, having just been sucked through a modified grain vacuum at roughly a hundred miles per hour. Tellis would insert the nozzle into one of their tunnels and the next thing you know there would be a solid *thwump*. They shot through the vortex, hitting the inside of the cage like a fastball hitting a catcher's mitt. Dave watched with both fascination and disgust.

'Doesn't this give them brain damage?'

'I am providing an environmental service.'

'They look a little concussed.'

'I am providing an environmental service.'

'I know what an environmental service is . . .'

'Do you?' *Thwump*. Another one shot into the cage. The result of this pneumatic disengagement was that each emergent critter now sported a bad seventies blow-dry look, like a miniature werewolf.

'I appreciate what you told my wife, but let's be truthful. You don't sell these to the Japanese.'

'Well you got me there.'

'What *do* you do with them?'

'Sell 'em to a medical lab. They use them to study the effects of head wounds on soldiers.'

'That's sick.'

Tellis cackled and slapped Dave on his shoulder.

'You bring a sense of humour when you moved here?'

'I have a sense of humour but you're not funny.'

Tellis gave Dave a black stare, a kind of telepathy that he wasn't to be fucked with.

'I wouldn't be doing this if your wife let you use a rifle,' he said.

'How do you know she won't?'

'She's afraid you'll hurt yourself.' The grin reappeared. He hung the coil on a pair of L-braces at the back of the cab and climbed back into the truck. Dave jumped on the running board. He didn't like the patronising nature of this skinny little shitstick one bit, his insinuation that he, Dave, wasn't exactly in the driver's seat of his own marriage. On top of this, the truck was carving up his freshly ploughed furrows. Tellis, far more perceptive than his indolent nature suggested, read this right away.

'You plantin' for winter wheat?' he called over the truck's grind.

'I am.'

'You playing at it or serious?'

'Why?'

'You ploughed in the wrong direction.'

'What do you mean?'

'What I mean is you went north–south. We get low winter sun here. You want your rows runnin' east–west.' In truth, it made no difference, but Tellis was a guy who viewed misinformation as a wonderful tool for manipulation.

He spotted another prairie dog mound and slammed to a stop, almost sending Dave off the running board. Tellis jumped out to inspect the hole. Dave followed behind him.

'How much do you know about wheat farming?' Dave said.

'Everything.'

'Maybe you could give me some more pointers,' Dave said.

'Sure. Here's one. For every nickel you put in, you lose a dime.'

'That's not true any more. I'm going to sell it for biofuel.'

'Bio-what?'

'Biofuel. Ethanol. Welcome to the oughts, friend.'

Tellis dismissed this explanation, saying that for two hundred years now folks had been thinking they'd get rich on grain.

'You can take a Sunday drive or eat toast,' he said. 'It don't matter. Wheat's just goddamned wheat.' He pulled a penlight from his pocket and knelt down. He shone the light into the tunnel, looking for the glimmer of tiny eyes. Then he stood back up and walked the length of the tunnel until he found its corresponding exit.

'Twelve feet,' he said. 'Figure a dog for every three feet. That's four prairie dogs.' He went over and flipped the compressor switch, then offered the nozzle to Dave.

'Wanna give it a shot?'

'No thanks.'

'That's what I thought.' Tellis pushed the nozzle into the hole. *Thwump. Thwump. Thwump. Thwump.*

'Now if you don't mind, I need to use your irrigation ditch to sump out.'

'How do you know there's a ditch?' said Dave. There *was* an irrigation ditch but you couldn't see it from where they stood.

'This is a ranch, ain't it?' said Tellis. He realised he needed to be careful about what he said to this man, about tipping his hand. There was an idea slowly formulating in his mind, but he wasn't real clear yet on how to work it.

They climbed back in and drove over the crest. The irrigation ditch was at the bottom of the middle pasture, running below a berm lined with chokecherry thickets. Tellis went to the headgate, opened it and let a stream of water rush in. He sucked it through his vacuum and then turned the hose on the cage, washing down the dust. Only then did he allow himself to see what he needed to see.

'I gotta piss,' he announced and walked to the far edge of the thicket. He unzipped and stood there peeing, looking into the undergrowth.

The sheep-herder's wagon was still there, practically obscured. Tellis could just make out the bowed roof and a stovepipe running out of an asbestos ring. The awning over the screened window had fallen off. Tellis felt a palpable childhood glow alight within him. Many years ago the wagon had contained his bunk, his fishing rods, his Winchester .22, his collection of Louis L'Amour novels, his biographies of Wyatt Earp, Jesse James, Lewis and Clark. He had practically lived there summers, only venturing up to his folks' house for replacements of canned food.

The wagon nestled in some faraway wash of memories. The prairie dogs, in the altogether here and now, clamoured over each other in their prison, trying to escape the magnifying effect of the sun's heat. These two sights, taken in together, were simultaneously familiar and wistful and suddenly seemed, to Tellis Wondersweet, to tie his future together.

He zipped up and walked back over to Dave Slocum. 'We're done here,' he said. 'Now I'd like to get paid.'

Humane virtues could not be ascribed to a man like Tellis Wondersweet, particularly because he had done time for manslaughter. This had happened in Arizona eight years earlier. He had left his folks' farm in Montana – the very one Dave and Marcie Slocum now owned – to run down the length of the Rockies searching for that apocryphal American West he'd always read about and not found a single detail of. Eventually he ended up sitting at a horseshoe-shaped bar in south Phoenix absently nursing his beer, staring not *at* but *beyond* some bikers across from him. One of them was a scrawny guy with a wild growth of facial hair, an attempt at a beard that looked as if he'd shoved his lips through some steel wool. Tellis's wayward stare was as close to a challenge as the biker was going to find that night.

'Sonofabitch you lookin' at?' he called, jarring Tellis out of his reverie. Tellis chose to ignore the comment, but fifteen minutes later when he tried to leave, the guy was outside, blocking his exit. The biker etched a line in the sand with his boot and invited Tellis to cross it. Tellis thought, *This is the kind of thing you only see in movies,* then the biker was on him. The ensuing scuffle was nothing more than an exchange of headlocks, clownishly choreographed. The two disengaged and stood glaring at each other, wondering who would make the next move. A small crowd had gathered. They wondered as well. The biker upped the stakes by producing a buck knife from a small leather case on his back hip. One of his buddies, a stocky fellow in a denim jacket, sidled up to Tellis and said under his breath, 'I'm a cop. Touch my hand and this bastard goes straight to jail.' In this odd pantomime, Tellis smelled collusion. He pulled the man's jacket back to find a nickel-plated .38 snubnose, snatched it from the man's waistband and shot the biker through the chest. It was as effortless as spraying a garden hose nozzle at a sapling. He walked to his car and drove straight to a strip club, where he sat waiting for the cops to arrive, thinking, *Where, from sea to shining sea, is the thing they call decency any more?* Back in Montana, bar fights were just a form of recreation, often ending in new-found friendships.

He did six remarkably uneventful years at the Maricopa Prison. When he emerged he was twenty-nine and rail thin with dark compression ridges under his eyes. Also, a soured attitude toward life. As far as he was concerned, the incident with the biker had been arguable self-defence. In the eyes of Arizona Law Enforcement, he was a cold-blooded murderer. The only thing the courts had left him was a hand-lacquered black 1968 Camaro. It had been seized by the State of Arizona for the length of his prison tenure and he was pretty sure someone had been driving it during that time. When it was returned to him it had a Right to Life bumper sticker and a pair of child safety seats in the back. He drove it home to his folks in Montana. Neither so much as hugged him, publicly shamed by his incarceration. His dad presented him with a signed deed to the farm. They had unloaded all but sixty acres. Ranching was a mug's game, his dad announced, an endless losing venture, you can have it. He informed Tellis that he and the Old Lady were retiring to Arizona. All Tellis could think to say about this circular turn of events was that Arizona was goddamn unbearable in the summer and they ought to consider central air-conditioning. That was the last he ever saw of them.

Tellis spent his days in a kind of crazy-lonely fog, which led to drinking, which led to a loss of temper with no one to take it out on. The farm implements gathered rust. An elevator full of durum seedlings collected mould. Somewhere in Brazil an intrepid team of ag-engineers were discovering that wheat-based biofuels provided an excellent alternative to corn: a development unnoticed by Montanans. The gradual gradation of a worldwide green revolution was slow to reach this part of the world, particularly to people like Tellis, part of that breed of miscreant Americans who, when the chips were down, took to viewing our shimmering republic through the bottom of a whisky glass. Somewhat rashly, he entered into a torturous sixty-three-day marriage to a skinny girl from Two Dot, which ended with the court reconciling her what remained of the ranch. The place had been in Tellis's family for four generations. She auctioned it off the following Saturday and left in the front seat of a Mayflower van, sitting close enough to the driver to make Tellis imagine they might be starting a new life together with all of his stuff

He began drinking suicidally, then stopped when he realised he'd never have the nerve to finish the job. Six years languishing in a sweltering correctional facility had done nothing to diminish the predominant revelation of his life: that he was effortlessly capable of killing someone else but not himself. You could now add to this a second revelation: he was dumber than a bag of wet mice.

He sobered up just lucidly enough to trade in the Camaro for the creaky flatbed Ford. On the back of this thing he built his prairie dog contraption.

Tellis drove all over south central Montana with those prairie dogs. Wherever he saw evidence of an infestation, he left a card in the owner's mailbox. Those who didn't know him invariably asked a reasonable question: *What the hell are you doing with all those prairie dogs?* To which he sarcastically replied, *They're going to open for the Pope on his next tour,* a sly Popemobile joke lost on most people in these parts, which was fine with Tellis, who had long ago tired of the question anyway. In slack moments he dreamed of getting his ranch back, of falling in love, of never having to suck another prairie dog out of the ground.

Tellis waited four days before driving back out to the Slocums' place late at night. He stopped the truck at the edge of the highway, alongside their pasture. The whole ride up there he had been trying to find the right word to explain the idea purring through his head, an idea as beautiful as the English gal in the house below him, the house that used to be his.

With surprising lightfootedness he scrambled down the short rampart leading to their front yard, avoided entanglement with a collection of Sears lawn chairs, shot across a travertine walkway and pivoted toward the side of the house. He crept along a row of rose trellises until he got to the window of the bedroom where a long line of Wondersweets had been conceived.

Dave Slocum was propped up in bed reading a copy of *Agrinews*. At the far end of the room Tellis observed Marcie at a small table in front of a make-up mirror. The soft glow of a wall sconce rendered her skin golden, almost wavering. She wore only a dark denim shirt, unbuttoned. Her slender fingers dug into a small white pot and began working something unguent from the proclivity of her neckbone downward in slow languid circles. Tellis found his breath coming in short gasps. He watched as the fingers worked their way further down, tantalisingly, a mock burlesque almost, until they reached the compact uplift of a pair of blushing . . . and that was it for Tellis, who grimly jetted a ropy helix of what Darwin had probably been referring to when he coined the term 'primordial ooze' on to the Slocum's roses.

Afterwards, he crept back to his truck, went around to the cage, opened it and watched the prairie dogs scamper into the moonlight.

He drove off slowly. It wasn't until he'd almost reached Pony, Montana, that the word came to him.

The word was *compensation*.

Marcie often felt as if she was sending a different Marcie out to deal with these Montanans, whose sensibilities appealed to her. These were people with hard lives, but who never foundered in their good nature. Imagining Britain now, she could only think of grey metallic sunsets, the wreck of human debris and the dreary tired line of failed socialism. She didn't miss it for a moment. Small, distinctly Montanan things thrilled her: the way drivers waved at each other on back roads. Or the way people stood by their word.

Tellis, for example, stood by his word.

He reappeared two days later. It couldn't have been at a more fortuitous moment. Dave was nowhere to be seen and Marcie's backside, buoyant, parabolic and altogether remarkable, was currently protruding from underneath the porch. Tellis took a moment to admire the way it pared down to slim ankles that he tried to envision locking around his back.

'Still sexy,' he whooped.

She crawled out to see who it was. He stood over her flashing his best Saturday-night smile, still old-school enough to believe a cowboy was any woman's weakness.

'Oh, hello.' She rubbed her forehead into her elbow and brushed away some dirt.

'What're you doing under the house?'

'There's a dog up under here. I think it's distressed.'

Tellis got down on his knees beside Marcie and peered, noting the heat from her torso and a fragrant whorl of moisturiser. Underneath the porch he could just make out a lumpen form. He got out his penlight and clicked it on, then stood up.

'What you got right there is a hound of some kind. Probably a Plott.'

'A Plott?'

'And it's met up with a porcupine.'

'Oh. Oh my.'

Wordlessly, Tellis went to his truck and came back wielding a length of pipe with a rope loop at one end: a device for extricating badgers.

The dog clearly needed help, going about it in a real unfriendly way. It took quite a bit of effort for Tellis to drag it out, straining against the loop with all its snarling, whimpering might. It was laced from muzzle to belly with quills. Tellis handed the badger stick to Marcie and told her to hold on tight. He went back to his truck for a tarp. The thing was taking Marcie around in circles: she looked like one of those hammer throwers in the Olympics. Tellis got the tarp over the dog, wrestled it down and rolled it up in the canvas until just its head protruded. He instructed Marcie to find a stick and wrap some duct tape around

136

it, and in this way made a crude bit that he could run through the dog's mouth to keep it from snapping at them. At this point the hound seemed to know the jig was up. The two of them plucked the quills from its muzzle, and by the time they were done, the creature had made up its mind about them. Tellis undid the canvas and the dog stood there acquiescent, letting them pull quills from its belly

'Looks like you got yourself a dog,' he said. 'You got any whisky?'

She went inside and came back out with some Jameson's. Tellis used some of it to clean out the dog's mouth, then started in on the rest. The crude gallantry of this whole episode was not lost on him. He invited himself inside.

'Good thing I showed up when I did, eh?' he said, leaning his frame against the kitchen counter.

'You want some coffee?' she asked. Tellis perceived, in this question, unabashed flirtation.

'Just whisky for me. Thanks!'

It was occurring to Marcie that in between prairie dogs and porcupine-riddled mutts, a localised natural horror was slowly unveiling itself. She was thankful Tellis had showed up and only wished he wasn't such a lurch. Often a man displaying signs of public crudity – drooling, drinking whisky in the middle of the afternoon, driving around with a giant box of omnivores – is actually, beneath the surface, suffering from something far more intricate. Marcie was compassionate enough to see this. Tellis saw quite another thing in Marcie and imagined the following conversation:

'Where's the hubby?'
'At work.'
'So you're sayin' afternoons are better for you?'

137

'That's exactly what I'm saying. Now spread me across this table and ride me like the cowboy you are before my husband Dave Slocum gets home.'

He watched her make the coffee, alternating between mentally undressing her and the very kitchen they stood in. His fondest recollections of this room were now debased by dismal veneer panelling. The linoleum was a repeating pattern of hapless escutcheons. There was a lurking dropped ceiling. He wasn't sure who had done this: the place had been through several owners since his mercenary ex-wife had liquidated it. Tellis suddenly felt a surge of apoplectic rage. He remembered oak floorboards and a great red cast-iron stove, his mom's cherry pies, the fruit culled from the orchard at the bottom of the yard, the blue curl of cigar smoke from his dad's ever-present Swisher Sweets: memories now ruthlessly violated by the kind of cheapjack frippery any asshole could scarf from a Home Depot bargain bin. It was goddamned heartbreaking.

Marcie poured herself a cup of coffee.

'Out of curiosity,' she asked, 'why did you show up?'

'Just makin' sure those prairie dogs didn't come back.'

'Funny that. They have.'

'Well they're known to fuck like crazy, if you'll pardon my salty vernacular.'

'I'm familiar with the term.'

'I'll bet you are.' For all the world this looked like an opening. 'Matter of fact, we could walk down to the fields and watch 'em.'

'I'll pass.'

'Who knows, some of it might rub off on you and me.'

'Not likely.'

'Oh, I get it. You're still in the throes of newly married. Still got that new car smell, eh? It's been my experience that lasts until about day sixty-three.'

'We're well past day sixty-three. But I'll let you know if anything changes, Mr Wondersweet.'

'Call me Tellis.'

'Tellis . . .'

''Cause once you've had a cowboy . . .'

'Where I'm from, *cowboy* is used to describe shoddy workmanship . . .'

'Me, I never been west of the Pecos . . .'

'. . . shysters . . .'

'But from what I've heard, you English gals are—'

'You can stop now, Tellis.'

'Sure thing. You gonna fix this place up?'

'Oh God,' she sighed. 'I don't even know where to begin. The couple we bought it from . . .' She stopped short, aware perhaps of denigrating otherwise decent people for their decorating skills.

'I can show you exactly where to start. You got any tools?'

She sent him out to the barn. He returned with a pickaxe, said, 'Allow me,' and with a dramatic flourish drove the business end of the thing right into the veneer, ripping it back to reveal perfect Swedish joinery: fat hand-peeled logs and mud chinking. In the four generations since a burgeoning sheep rancher named Claude Vernal Wondersweet had assembled them, the logs had acquired a dull grey patina. Tellis took a sheet of No. 4 sandpaper, and worked it briskly across a log, and observed in Marcie's face sheer delight. The log shone with that rustic nouveau quality that makes decorators collectively cream their designer jeans.

Within an hour, the two of them had the panelling off and piled in the middle of the room. Tellis got Marcie to pour some linseed oil on to a rag and he wiped it over a log. The resultant glow, he noted gleefully, corresponded

139

to the one on Marcie's face, and he envisioned for just a moment her throwing herself on top of him. Behind her in the kitchen window, Dave's face appeared, gaped, then vanished. Then he was in the doorway, his lips tight against his teeth, surveying the demolished kitchen.

'Can you believe it?' said Marcie. 'This is an original homestead.'

'What's he doing back here?' he said to Marcie.

'Dave. I'm standin' right here.'

'All right. What are you doing here?'

'I told you I come with a guarantee.'

'The prairie dogs are back,' Marcie volunteered.

Dave took the whisky bottle from Tellis. 'I've spent the day watching a foursome of drunken Kiwanis louts turn my fairway into Swiss cheese,' he said measuredly. 'Two seventy-year-old ladies complained there was a sulphur smell coming up from the water hazards.' He went to a shelf, found a glass, and poured himself a drink. 'Then I receive a visit from a patron of the Ruby Valley Preservation Society who informs me my par-three track is situated over sacred Crow burial grounds. At the end of the day, my greenskeeper finds empty miniature liquor bottles in every cup.' He took a drink and stared blackly at Tellis. 'Then I come home to this. Who does that mangy dog belong to, by the way?'

'Other than that, honey,' said Tellis, 'how was your day?'

Marcie tried to stifle a laugh at this. Dave glared at her, then back at Tellis.

'Get rid of those goddamned prairie dogs.'

Tellis revacuumed the pastures, thinking about the couple in the house. In Dave he saw an inferior version of himself. In Marcie he saw something strong and compassionate and peerless and wondered why it couldn't have been a woman like that who'd ruined him instead of an anorexic bumpkin from Two Dot. From the seat of his truck he peered down with avaricious eyes at land that had once been his, his brain firing a direct linkage of images: the long-lost souls of his grandparents and great-grandparents who'd tried beyond all means to stretch more out of this place than it could possibly offer up: the burrowing of the intransigent *Cynomys ludovicianus*; the interment of Crows, callously disregarded by the men in lime-green golf trousers who trod over their ghosts. Every being, thought Tellis, was entitled to its ancestral ground, a continuum that included one Telford C. Wondersweet, currently of no fixed address, unless you counted the Comfort Inn of Ennis, where he was currently being dunned for two months' back rent.

With the prairie dogs once again dislodged, he trundled down to the headgate to hose down the truck. Sixty, maybe seventy prairie dogs glowered back at him, as if to let him know they were getting pretty goddamn sick of this whole routine. Then Tellis went to the sheepherder's wagon, clambered through the undergrowth and had a look inside.

All manner of rodentia had had their way with the interior. There were mouldering piles of dead flies and spent .22 casings. Tellis found a gnawed paperback lying in the corner: Louis L'Amour's *How the West Was Won*. He sat on the edge of a thoroughly masticated bunk and thumbed through the passage where Linus Rawling, who'd wandered the wilderness for twenty-odd years, falls in love with a woman he's only known for a couple of days. Implausible, thought Tellis, with the dispiriting realisation that he'd spent a good part of his youth swallowing this kind of rubbish hook, line and sinker. His thoughts drifted toward the house above him. Question: was Marcie good-looking? Tellis had always preferred skinny woman, Marcie wasn't skinny, but by no means was she big. She was slender and long, but what impressed you about her, aside from those undulating orbs of course, was her eyes, which seemed wide open and attentive to everything. Also her accent, which just reeked of exoticness and made Tellis, by association, feel worldlier. He reminded himself to find out where, exactly, Britain was on the map. He was thinking that the sooner he could get Dave out of the picture, the sooner they'd ... well, just pretty much travel the world together.

A shadow crossed the page. He looked up and saw Dave's face at the wagon entrance.

'I was just going through my deed contracts,' he said. 'Wouldn't you know, the name Wondersweet figures prominently in the owner history.'

'Figured that out on your own, didya?'

'You're a shabby, shabby man, Tellis.'

'Back off. I'm comin' out.'

Dave made no effort to move.

'You opened up the whole can of worms with your little stunt in the kitchen. She won't stop now until that entire place is done up.'

'That's women for you.'

'I don't have the time or the money.'

'Gotta keep a smile on their face.'

'You I want off this property.'

'Or what?'

'Or what?'

'You gonna shoot me, Dave?'

'No, I'm not going to shoot you. I'm going straight to the county sheriff.'

'Well now, that just degrades all parties involved.'

'Yes, but they provide a public service. And I'm a taxpayer.'

'I got a better idea.'

'What's that?'

'You take me on.'

'What?'

'A ranch hand type deal. You don't mind my sayin', you're in way over your head.'

'You don't know a goddamned thing what I'm about.'

'Yeah? You know how to run a swather? Spray Malathion? What are you gonna do you get aphids, curlmites, mosaic . . . every other visitation written up in your monthly copy of *Agrinews*? I get the impression from your old lady she won't stand for a man who don't know what he's doin'.'

'Don't ever mention my wife again.'

'Here's the deal, Dave. I'm gonna bunk in right down here, bring in your wheat, run this spread the way it needs to be run. You get out those tools in your barn and start in on the house . . .'

'Here's why that won't work. I don't like you.'

'That part works itself out. You'll see.'

'Get off my property.' He cleared the doorway, an invitation for Tellis to leave.

'Fine,' grunted Tellis and climbed down from the wagon. He sauntered past Dave to his truck, pausing beside the prairie dogs.

'I'm a goddamn cowboy!' he called out. 'What your historians call a dyin' breed!'

'I'm not interested in anthropology, Mr Wondersweet.'

'Yeah, well we'll be seein' each other,' he said, and disappeared into his truck cab.

*   *   *

Bugs swarmed under the floodlights of the Ennis Golf Club, where a lone disconsolate figure named Carl Steagall could be seen gathering up stray balls with a claw device and dropping them into an apron. Carl was the club's concessions manager, greenskeeper and sometimes-caddy. In fact he was Dave Slocum's only employee. He wore bib overalls and scuffed along in a way that made it clear he despised golfing and all that went along with it, retrieving each ball with the loathsome demeanour of someone picking up dog turds.

Tellis, watching from the highway, lit a cigarette and felt a flush of high spirits. He had a clear-eyed view of how things went from here. He watched as Carl worked his way back toward the driving platform and, when the last of the balls were gathered, disappeared into the shadows of the concession shack.

A few moments later the floodlights shut down. Tellis stubbed out his cigarette and went around to the back of the truck. A hoary team chant ran through his head, a kind of smug joke: *Who let the dawgs out?*

He unlocked the cage. The prairie dogs poured out and headed straight for the driving range and the great carpet of fairway beyond. They scampered, stopped, scampered, looked around, whistled to each other, fathoming the enormity of this new and green green glorious home. Then they began tunnelling.

By the following day a golfer no longer knew which *hole* to putt his ball into. Dave endured a litany of complaints, apologised profusely and shelled out refunds. At closing time, he told Carl Steagall he would see him next April and shut down early for the season.

Winter came as a series of blustery leaden cold fronts. Wind tore through the holes in the house where the chinking had crumbled.

At night Dave lay awake beside Marcie and listened to the howling, feeling the warmth radiating from her back. He laid his face in the small channel of her shoulder blades and wrapped her thick curly hair around her neck so he could look out the window at the telephone poles silhouetted against the highway. Some nights he was certain he could make out Tellis's truck parked up there.

One day in November the phone rang. Dave picked it up and heard Tellis's flat drawl on the other end.

'How's it hangin', chief?'

'You put those goddamn prairie dogs on my golf course, didn't you?'

'That's a disturbing insinuation.'

'What do you want?'

'I thought maybe you'd changed your mind. About my offer.'

'I haven't.'

'I could drive out your place, sandblast them logs for you. My rig's set up for that sort of thing.'

'I'm doin' fine, Tellis.'

'Tell me you're not trying to do it by hand.'

'They're comin' along.'

'You'll be at it till Jesus gets back.'

'That's my problem.'

'I'm just tryin' to be normal, Dave. Just offerin' my help. Eight hours to do what it'll take you all winter to do by hand.'

'I'll think about it.'

'All right. How's the dog?'

'Good. Real good. Thanks for askin'.'

'A dog like that needs special care.'

'Thanks.'

'Well, I'll be talkin' to you.'

145

Dave hung up. Marcie was standing under the living room arch, looking at him.

'What did he want?' she asked.

'Work.'

'You ought to consider it. He knows this house inside and out.'

'So do the termites.'

Dave had been right about one thing: restoring the house to its homestead condition became, for Marcie, a patent obsession. She would stand in each room and describe a verbal picture of what she desired, of sunny recesses, basking floorboards, chrome plumbing and spiffy new fixtures: a house that glowed.

Dave withered at each suggestion. The more things he ripped from the bowels of the place and piled in the yard – wiring, plumbing, chinking, insulation – the more he saw how dire was the place's true condition, such was the cancerous nature of remodelling. Spavined, he drove to the bank in Ennis.

The loan officer, Don Macumber, was a small, harried-looking man who clearly had more important things to do with his afternoon.

'Go ahead,' he said, when Dave had taken a seat in an uncomfortable chair across from his desk. From the window behind Don's desk, Dave could look out to the edge of town and see his perforated golf course, under a blanket of fresh snow.

'I need a home improvement loan.'

'Who's doing the remodelling?'

'I am.'

'Do you know what you're doing?'

'I intend to figure it out.'

Macumber pulled his face to one side and eyed Dave.

'As a rule, we only make rcmodelling loans if you got a professional contractor in place. I can recommend a few.'

'Like I said, I think I can do it on my own.'

'What you got in the way of collateral?'

'I own the golf club here in town.'

Macumber's eyes widened. Then he checked his watch and dropped his elbows to his desk.

'Sure. I can give you the loan.'

'That's good.'

'Unfortunately you'll need signed approval from your co-owners.'

'What co-owners?'

'A couple hundred dead Crow Indians.'

Dave came home and laid out his tools on the kitchen table, where the light was good and the coffee was close. But he knew it was all hopeless and he put them away again and picked up the phone and called Tellis Wondersweet.

An hour later Tellis pulled up in his contraption. Dave was waiting for him in the driveway. In that moment, an arc of mutuality as could only be produced by two hopelessly inconvenienced men crossed from one to the other.

Tellis insinuated himself into their lives as if he now owned them. In a way he did. He moved his belongings into the sheep-herder's wagon and took over the restoration project, blasting the old bark off the logs until they glowed and seemed to give off their own golden light. He replaced the crumbly chinking with some kind of miraculous, possibly carcinogenic expanding foam. The stuff came in aerosol containers. Dave marvelled at how compressed it was, like someone had stuffed a bouncy

147

castle into a can. Tellis mitred with precision, kept every-thing straight and true and level. He built new cupboards from white pine, rewired the entire house, restored the dropped ceiling to its original height. Often he and Marcie worked side by side, talking animatedly to each other. The leering, wolfish qualities he first exhibited had now modulated to something almost like possession. They had enthusiasm and a shared goal. Dave felt consigned to the margins. He was constantly sent to the hardware store or lumberyard for supplies. Their small savings were running out fast, but Marcie only seemed to want to see beyond that.

'I feel like an errand boy,' he said one night as they lay in bed.

'You are.'

'What's happened to you, Marcie?'

'Nothing's happened to me. I want a nice home.'

'So do I, but this is bleeding me dry.'

'If this is all too much for you . . .'

'What. What's that mean?'

'It means take it serious, Dave.'

'Serious*ly*.'

'What?'

'You said *take it serious*. Three months ago you would have said *seriously*. Where are you getting this locution?'

She turned out the light. A minute later, from the dark, she said:

'We ought to let him stay in the guest bedroom. He must be freezing down there.'

They stopped having sex. He knew Marcie adored him, but he was too financially preoccupied to fulfil what she considered a small but important part of their life together. She was full of a wanton electricity and he could not help but think she was being drawn to Tellis, though he couldn't for the life of him understand quite why. Perhaps it was just the way he strove to pay attention to her.

In the spring, when the new wheat was at ankle height, Dave felt a slight sense of relief. It seemed to represent some kind of financial salvation.

Marcie had planted a garden out behind the house. He paid her endeavour little attention: he was far more worried about how he was going to get the wheat out of the ground. He didn't own a combine, nor did he feel familiar enough with his neighbours to ask for their help. He had a frightening image of himself and Tellis standing side by side, like a pair of cowboy grim reapers, scything it up by hand.

One morning she walked him out and showed him what she had done. An urgent-looking hummingbird vibrated before them as they walked down the path. It almost felt like a Disney moment. The garden was warm under the morning sun. Dave wondered briefly what ghosts lay under this freshly tilled soil. She showed him how things were arranged, the peppers, the staked tomatoes, the new melons glistening under dew. He was thrilled. All this emerging life seemed like a beacon of things working themselves out. But then Marcie announced that her mother had taken ill back in England, and she needed to go home. Dave stared off, with a sudden feeling of nausea. She kept talking, explaining the specifics of the malaise, using words like 'migrating' and 'exploratory', but Dave couldn't quite focus on what she was saying. He was stuck on the way she had used the word *home. I need to go home.*

They couldn't afford the round-trip ticket to London. Marcie called her father, who arranged for a wire transfer. Dave felt as if his heart was coated with ice. That afternoon he sat on the edge of the bed in their fresh new bedroom and silently watched her pack. Her hair was up in a kind of tight hive and she wore a green Western shirt with black roses at the yoke. When she was done, she said, 'I need to go down and talk to Tellis.'

'Okay,' he answered. She brushed by him. There was nothing funny or suspicious in this. He wandered to the kitchen, mechanically turned on the coffee machine and made a fresh pot, looking out the window at his wife moving across the top pasture, the Plott hound loping ahead, until they both disappeared down the slope. He put some non-dairy creamer into his coffee and stared at it. It didn't seem to want to mix, just making strange floating shapes on the surface.

He stood at the window for a long time, though he couldn't be sure exactly how long that time was. Eventually the dog reappeared at the crest of the hill, then a moment later, Marcie, her hair trailing behind her like smoke. He watched as she stopped momentarily, pulled what must have been bobby pins from her teeth, flounced her hair and pinned it back up.

The following day he drove her to the airport. The place was crammed with local college kids heading out on spring break. They bustled with inchoate energy, all base-ball caps and bulging knapsacks. Dave marvelled at how casually self-contained they seemed: turtles with iPods. A massive cast-bronze statue of a grizzly bear dominated the departure lounge, its claws extended in a gesture that seemed somehow half threatening, half welcoming.

'You never asked me to come with you,' Dave said.

'Because I knew you wouldn't. Right?'

'Yeah.'

'You think I've quit, don't you?'

'I don't know what you're thinking.'

'I'm going to miss you,' she said. Dave felt something very close to collapse in his life now. But he refused to show it and just pulled her to him. She buried her face in his shoulder and said: 'Something's gotta give.'

Then she was walking away. He called out something hoarse and stricken to her. Anyone standing close enough to hear would probably have imagined it was 'Bye, I love you.' But it would have been hard to be certain. Maybe what he said was 'biofuel'.

Afterwards he drove to the golf course and parked at the concession shack. He climbed into an electric cart and drove around the grounds, taking in the damage. He felt dazed and heavy. *Is it instinct or memories that keep us going?* he wondered to himself, and tried to envision, in a nonspecific and slightly narcotic way, life without Marcie.

He found Carl Steagall hovering over a spring that fed the small pond near the ninth hole. Carl had a .22 rifle with a Bushnell scope strapped across his back. He greeted Dave like he'd only seen him yesterday.

'Look at this,' he said. Dave climbed out and went over. There were some old cartridges lying in the grass: rusty 45–70s.

'Coulda been a fight,' Carl pondered. 'Or maybe a soldier shooting deer. But they're definitely from a cavalry rifle.' He reached down to pick one up. A good part of Carl Steagall's life involved picking things up from the ground.

Dave said, 'Leave 'em. It's someone's history.'

Carl stood back up. 'Suit yourself.'

A sudden shadow crossed the thick grass about ten yards away. In the time it took Dave to recognise it as a prairie dog, Carl had already plugged it. The thing clutched

151

its chest like a hamfisted actor, staggered a few inches and dropped. Carl walked over, inspected it with the toe of his boot, and kicked it back into its tunnel.

Out of the blue, Dave said, 'What is it that keeps us going, Carl?'

Carl looked at him strangely.

'Say what?'

'What is it that keeps us going?'

Carl stared down at the prairie dog corpse for a while. Then he shrugged and said, 'I don't know. If I was pushed for an answer, I'd say bran muffins.' He handed the .22 to Dave.

'See what you can do with this. I gotta mow.'

Dave spent the rest of the afternoon shooting prairie dogs. At first he felt a little queasy, but by the fourth kill he was definitely experiencing a crude adrenalised rush: what people call 'bloodlust'. He piled the carcasses next to the flag at the ninth hole.

By the time he got home, a violet dusk was gathering at the edge of the Tobacco Roots. He had Carl's .22 lying across the back seat of the car. It was his favourite time of day, that interval when welcoming illumination shifts from the big sky to the windows of houses standing stark against the receding West.

He sat there staring at the house. He couldn't seem to take his eyes off of it, its memories, its betrayal and the great distance beyond.

Eventually the kitchen door opened and Tellis Wondersweet appeared. He leaned against the door frame in a square of light, smoking a cigarette and rubbing his thumb against his index finger. He slowly extended the finger outward, studying it as if there might be a splinter there he would never remove.

He is in our house and our house is in him, Dave thought to himself.

He climbed out of the car.

Neither really desired a showdown: the Great Montana Saga is one of give and take, necessity and reciprocal back-scratching. He got the gun from the back seat, and squared up to Tellis with that same tension that had visited so many men before them.

Ultimately, the two arrived at an agreement.

emily's arrival

E-GRATULATIONS! ANNOUNCING the arrival of our
PRIDE, our JOY, our NEW WALLPAPER.
(PHOTO OF BABY GIRL)
EMILY ROSARIO PERLMUTTER
BORN: ?? 2007 in GUATEMALA
ARRIVED HOME: 25 January, 2008 to the loving
carbon-neutral arms of WENDY and ROSS PERLMUTTER

Isn't she precious? Please note that the grey shading in
the picture is a result of conversion for viewing on your
screen and in no way represents Emily's true pigmenta-
tion. If you wish to print off Emily's pic, *please, please*
use recyclable paper.

ABOUT HER NATURAL PARENTS

All I can say is Emily now has a real family, not a pretend
one. Nothing against the Guatemalans (those pan-flute

bands are amazing), but whereas her real mother gave her a nationality, we are here to give her the World . . . and to teach her how to protect it!

A FUTURE FOR OUR CHILD

Every child, no matter how precious, leaves a teensy-tiny carbon footprint. During adoption proceedings, Ross and I made seven round-trip flights to Guatemala City. Calculated at five tons of CO_2 emissions per person per trip[*] that comes out at . . . well, *you* do the math . . . seventy tons! To give you an idea of how much CO_2 that is, imagine drinking 64,000 Pepsis (Diet *or* Regular) a day for the rest of your life. Thus you can see that Emily arrives in this world with quite a substantial CO_2 debt on her little shoulders. Let's start planting those trees, people!

A VISIT

Emily can't wait to see all her new friends and admirers! We strongly insist that if you plan to pay a visit, please 'green' it. Car-pooling is highly recommended. Ross is organising a VanPool (hybrid eight-seater) for next Tuesday, 1 February, at 4:00 p.m. Just let us know if you want a ride.

GIFTS

Riddle: what kind of showers don't carry acid rain? Answer: baby showers! (LOL.) They can, however, impact

[*] The five tons of CO_2 per person is a conservative estimate based on a full plane. In fact, the flights we took *to* Guatemala City were only half full, so a truer calculation would be 7.5 tons of CO_2 emissions per person. However, Ross and I are not going to accept undue blame. It's not our fault if Guatemala City is a shithole and no one wants to fly there!

on nature in other insidious ways, so be very careful what you choose to bring as a gift. No gratuitous wrapping paper, ribbons or bows, please. I don't need to tell you what *that's* doing to our forests. We recommend 100 per cent cotton clothing, dye-free, and of course any baby-wear made from recyclable products. No Nike or Baby Gap stuff. The jury's still out on their 'fair-trade' claims. We really want to keep little Emily logo-free. And oh yes, Gina Ford books are strictly no-go in our household. That woman's murdered a lot of trees with her Nazi child-rearing manifestos.

In fact we would like to suggest a wonderful alternative: Ross has set up a carbon-offset account in Emily's name. Why not forgo those Teletubbies and fluffy booties and make a donation in Emily's name to the Vivo Project of Uganda, which is currently attempting to build a wood-fired biomass boiler that operates on a thirty-kilowatt photovoltaic turbine system!! Little Emily will love you for it!

THE BIG QUESTION: CLOTH VS DISPOSABLE

Ross and I have agonised endlessly over what kind of impact Emily's nappy usage (a period we conservatively estimate to be two and a half years) will have on the environment. Obviously we will eschew disposable diapers, given that a billion trees per year are cut down to make the wood pulp for disposables, not to mention the fact that the bleach used to whiten them produces organochlorine (dioxin: the primary ingredient of Agent Orange! And you thought baby poop was toxic!).

Unfortunately, cloth diapers, though recyclable, utilise a large number of pesticides and chemicals to harvest the cotton they're made from. Even more detrimentally, washing them would use approximately 30,000 gallons of water annually – a cumulative total of 75,000 gallons of water. My what a dilemma! After some serious back and forth on the issue, we realised maybe introspection was the answer: physician heal thyself, if you will. By calculating that Ross and I personally flush about 60,000 gallons per year down the toilet, the solution became obvious: all three of us are going to wear cloth diapers for the next two and a half years. By our calculations, this will result in a net gain of 90,000 gallons of water per year.

A FEW FINAL WORDS

Having endured fourteen failed *in vitros*, Ross and I were having a tough time understanding what was happening to us. We felt Nature had singled us out for punishment. We now appreciate that Ross's nugatory sperm yield was not a cruel twist of Nature, but in fact a Hidden Blessing (though I still maintain it's the result of a lifetime of ingested pollutants and industrial effluvia on Ross's part). The Adoption Process, for us, was clearly meant to be. Parenthood is a path, no matter how one arrives at it, though we both could have done with a little less paperwork and a more expeditious delivery. I know you're all sick of seeing us in those matching 'Expecting from Guatemala' T-shirts. Take our word for it . . . the wait was worth it!

musical ephemera

MEMOIRS OF ELLIS TINSLEY (THE DESK CLERK AT THE HEARTBREAK HOTEL)

N O QUESTION ABOUT it, it was Elvis who put us on the map. He used to stay here when he needed a break from Graceland. Used to say it was because his baby had left him, but I don't think that was really the case. His house was always crawling with decorators and I think they used to drive him a little crazy. He'd show up with a passel of hangers-on, yes-men, pals, what-have-you. They'd rent out the whole top floor and liked to run me ragged.

It's true I always dressed in black. But it ain't because I was gloomy. I thought it was just a smart way to look. Hell, nowadays all your swank hotels make their staff wear black. I was just ahead of the times, that's all. Elvis dug it.

'Lookin' good, Ellis!' he'd say whenever he saw me and shake my hand. Then he'd tip me a Cadillac.

There's a few other things need clearing up about that song. First of all, it wasn't called the Heartbreak Hotel and it wasn't down at the end of Lonely Street. It was the Harbrick Hotel and it was down at the end of Longley Street, just off Beale. I guess Elvis just took a little poetic licence with the name.

Yes, we were always crowded. We offered reasonable rates and we were family-friendly. There was a small swimming pool and a twenty-four-hour restaurant. Elvis never ate there, though. He knew regular folks wouldn't never be able to eat their dinners if they saw him in there, so with him it was strictly room-service.

'Send me up a fried pb&j with bananas, Ellis,' he'd say over the phone, and I'd have it up there pronto and he'd tip me a Cadillac. He'd invite me in for a chat. I know he liked to claim he was a little-less-conversation kind of guy, but he could talk a blue streak if you caught him in the right mood.

One time I asked him, 'Elvis, you know how in your movies you're always standing on a beach singing to a gal?'

He said, 'Unhunh.'

'And then the Jordanaires materialise behind you with electric guitars?'

'Unhunh.'

'Well, where does the power come from? For those guitars?'

He thought about that for a long time. Then he said, 'Unhunh.'

That's the kind of guy he was.

Elvis's favourite meal was breakfast. Lord, that man could put it away: a half-dozen fried eggs, ham fried in lard, biscuits with red-eye gravy, hash browns, a couple of fried green tomatoes, six pancakes with maple syrup, a pork chop, toast, a jar of peanut butter and a dozen Krispy Kreme doughnuts. And juice. Never coffee. Said caffeine always made him feel like someone was pushing him.

'No coffee, Ellis,' he'd warn me. 'Makes me feel like someone's pushin' me.' I wouldn't bring him any coffee and he'd tip me a Cadillac.

Afterwards he'd just lay there on the bed for two, three hours, unable to move. In the song he claims he was lyin' there in the gloom, lonely and heartbroken. But I think it was gastric distress. Elvis was never able to distinguish between the effects of heartbreak and a hearty breakfast.

I guess the truest thing about that song was how he claimed I was never going back. That's practically verbatim.

'Ellis, you been down here so long on Lonely (*sic*) Street, you ain't never going back,' he used to say. That was his joke.

I'd say, 'You got that right, Elvis.' He'd slap me on the shoulder blades and then . . . well, you guessed it.

Lord, that man liked to give away Cadillacs. He tipped me so many, I was able to open up my own dealership over in West Memphis. I got someone to run it for me and stayed right where I was . . . behind the desk of the Harbrick Hotel. For a while Elvis was even buying all his Cadillacs from my dealership and then tippin' 'em back to me. What a sweet racket.

Brother, those were the days.

DEATH OF THE GAMBLER

TRANSCRIPT OF ELECTRONIC INTERVIEW
CD NO.: WAV 2341071314136
ALLEGED IDENTITY OF PARTY: Kenny ROGERS

INTERVIEWING OFFICER: FEDERAL
AGENT Henry W. BURLE

AGENT BURLE: How you doin', Kenny? You don't mind I call you Kenny, do you?

KENNY ROGERS: Suit yourself.

AGENT BURLE: 'Suit yourself.' That's very nice of you. What did I say to the precinct chief before I came in here? I said, 'I bet this Kenny Rogers is a nice guy. I bet this Kenny Rogers is a hundred per cent team player.'

KENNY ROGERS: You're being sarcastic, aren't you?

AGENT BURLE: Me? Never.

KENNY ROGERS: They've sent you in here to bust my balls.

AGENT BURLE: I'm a straight-up kind of guy . . . what about you? You a straight-up guy?

KENNY ROGERS: I've already told the police everything I know!

AGENT BURLE: Well there's just a few . . . uh . . . discrepancies I'd like to clear up before we can . . . You mind I turn on this tape recorder? My memory ain't so good. Maybe I should eat more blueberries. I hear they're good for memory.

KENNY ROGERS: Maybe I should have my lawyer present.

AGENT BURLE: Now come on, Kenny. You only need a lawyer for a formal statement. And you'd only need to make a formal statement if you thought you were in trouble. Do you think you're in trouble, Kenny?

KENNY ROGERS: I haven't done anything.

AGENT BURLE: Of course you haven't. This is all purely . . . clerical. What interests me . . . what I'm curious about is the victim . . . I'm sorry . . . the deceased's final moments. Can you recall the last thing he said to you?

162

KENNY ROGERS: Yeah. He said, 'You gotta know when to hold 'em, know when to fold 'em, know when to walk away and know when to run . . .'

AGENT BURLE: *Did* he attempt to walk away?

KENNY ROGERS: No . . .

AGENT BURLE: To run?

KENNY ROGERS: Where would he run to? We were on a train.

AGENT BURLE: But why would a man say something like that if he didn't feel threatened? A man doesn't talk about running away unless he fears for his life . . .

KENNY ROGERS: He was talking about cards! He was being metaphorical!

AGENT BURLE: Oh, right. Metaphor. You sure like your metaphors, don't you, Kenny.

KENNY ROGERS: Yes, I do. In fact I'm probably as metaphorical as you are sarcastic.

AGENT BURLE: So . . . hold 'em, fold 'em . . . blah de blah . . . anything else? He say anything else?

KENNY ROGERS: He said, '. . . ev'ry hand's a winner and ev'ry hand's a loser . . . and the best that you can hope for is to die in your sleep . . .'

AGENT BURLE: 'Die in your sleep'? He actually said those words?

KENNY ROGERS: He did.

AGENT BURLE: Interesting. What happened then?

KENNY ROGERS: When he'd finished speakin', he turned back toward the window, crushed out his cigarette and faded off to sleep . . .

AGENT BURLE: And . . . ?

KENNY ROGERS: Somewhere in the darkness the gambler he broke even . . .

AGENT BURLE: 'Broke even'? The word we like to use around here is 'died'.

KENNY ROGERS: Well, yes. Died.

AGENT BURLE: I'm glad we're clear on that. Anyway . . . let's back up for a minute. Let's go over the events leading up to the victim's demise. According to your . . . uh . . . testimony . . . it was a warm summer's evening and you were on a train bound for nowhere?

KENNY ROGERS: Correct.

AGENT BURLE: So the train wasn't moving?

KENNY ROGERS: I was speaking figuratively. Meaning, the train was bound for nowhere special. Somewhere . . . you know . . . forgettable . . .

AGENT BURLE: Just another no-name town?

KENNY ROGERS: Yeah, exactly.

AGENT BURLE: So you're a bit of a drifter?

KENNY ROGERS: I suppose you could say that. Or you could say I'm just someone not averse to absorbing experience.

AGENT BURLE: Unh-hunh. I think I'm gonna go with drifter. Believe me, I know what it's like to hand-to-mouth it. I used to hitchhike a bit myself. Anyhoo . . . says here you met up with a gambler.

KENNY ROGERS: Right.

AGENT BURLE: So this was a prearranged meeting. You knew the victim?

KENNY ROGERS: No. I didn't know him. I just happened to sit next to him on the train. Met up just scans nicely.

AGENT BURLE: Does what?

KENNY ROGERS: Ewwww . . . it's a song-writing thing . . . it's hard to explain.

AGENT BURLE: Well, you need to try. Because quite frankly, Kenny, what I need from you right now is absolute clarity. You said you were both too tired to sleep . . . that you two took turns starin' out the window at the darkness.

164

KENNY ROGERS: Correct.

AGENT BURLE: So what's that exactly? He would look out the window for a while, then say, 'Okay, it's your turn to look out the window'?

KENNY ROGERS: We weren't *looking* for anything. We were just—

AGENT BURLE: My line of work we call that a stakeout. You then go on to say, 'till boredom overtook us and he began to speak'.

KENNY ROGERS: I suppose I was bored . . . It was a train . . . what's there to do on a train?

AGENT BURLE: Yeah . . . yeah . . . yeah . . . you said that. But you've admitted you're a bored drifter. That's a profile quite a few notable guys have fitted . . .

KENNY ROGERS: What guys?

AGENT BURLE: Oh, I don't know . . . guys like Charlie Starkweather. Leopold and Loeb. Rootless, idle types . . .

KENNY ROGERS: Whoa . . .

AGENT BURLE: Anything for kicks types. Guys just looking for that next jolt of adrenalin, that headrush that comes with the murdering of an innocent stranger.

KENNY ROGERS: Murder! Are you saying I murdered—

AGENT BURLE: Did I say that, Kenny? Did I say you murdered anyone? We were talking about Charlie Starkweather.

KENNY ROGERS: I think maybe I should have a lawyer . . .

AGENT BURLE: Well, well . . . allofasudden Mr Bored Drifter is concerned with his rights. Tell me about what the Gambler said to you.

KENNY ROGERS: Why? So you can twist—

AGENT BURLE: I'll tell you what he said. He said, 'Son, I've made a life out of readin' people's faces . . . blah dee . . . blah dee . . . you don't mind my sayin', I can see

you're out of aces . . . For a taste of your whiskey . . .'
So you admit to drinking at the time?

KENNY ROGERS: Yeah, I was drinking . . .

AGENT BURLE: And you coerced him into sharing . . .

KENNY ROGERS: I didn't coerce him. He said, 'For a taste of your whiskey I'll give you some advice.'

AGENT BURLE: And?

KENNY ROGERS: And what?

AGENT BURLE: What happened next?

KENNY ROGERS: So I handed him my bottle and he drank down my last swallow. Then he bummed a cigarette and asked me for a light. And the night got deathly quiet and his face lost all expression. He said, 'If you're gonna play the game, boy, you gotta learn to play it right.'

AGENT BURLE: Whoa, back up . . . what kind of quiet?

KENNY ROGERS: Deathly quiet.

AGENT BURLE: I see. But the man wasn't dead, was he? Not yet, anyway. And yet in your mind, it was 'deathly' quiet . . . the kind of quiet that precipitates death.

KENNY ROGERS: You're doing it again. Twisting my words.

AGENT BURLE: I'm just saying it's a very unusual choice of word to describe quiet. But then you're a very unusual man, Kenny. I mean, you're a man who doesn't care where he's going or where he's been. Who likes to get a little drunk on public transport, maybe coerce an old man into drinking with him . . .

KENNY ROGERS: He *asked* for a drink! There was no *coercion* . . .

AGENT BURLE: Pretty soon the talk gets around to cards . . . maybe a little hand of poker breaks out . . .

KENNY ROGERS: That's not true!

AGENT BURLE: Maybe somebody sees somebody counting their money . . .

KENNY ROGERS: That never happened.

AGENT BURLE: No, of course not. Now here's something you said really baffles me. 'In his final words I found an ace that I could keep.' You say that?

KENNY ROGERS: I did.

AGENT BURLE: You removed a playing card from the victim?

KENNY ROGERS: No. Metaphorically. Wisdom!

AGENT BURLE: Why would you do that? I'll tell you why. Because every pyscho creep sadistic murdering bastard needs a trophy . . .

KENNY ROGERS: That's not true . . .

AGENT BURLE: . . . to prolong, even nourish, the memory of his crime. To play over and over in his sick mind.

KENNY ROGERS: I want my lawyer.

AGENT BURLE: Oh, you're gonna need a lot more than a lawyer, Kenny. You're gonna need a really sympathetic jury. Maybe one that understands all your little metaphors. Guys like you make me sick. We're done here. (END OF RECORDING)

REQUEST DENIED

Office of the City Council

Mr Tony Orlando   June 14
Unit 23, Cellblock 4
State Correctional Facility

Mr Orlando,

After considerable deliberation the City Council
has voted overwhelmingly to deny your request to

tie a yellow ribbon around the Old Oak Tree. The Old Oak Tree is a venerable part of this town's history and decorating it is traditionally reserved for civic celebrations such as the Fourth of July or Christmas. We do not view your release from the State Correctional Facility as a cause for fanfare.

We appreciate that you've 'done your time'. Though you may well believe you've repaid your debt to society, we do not share your enthusiasm. In the eyes of the law, you are still a convicted criminal. Calling attention to your past misconduct by decorating a tree is, frankly, an insult to decent law-abiding citizens. May we suggest you try and reintegrate yourself into society as quietly as possible. Or even better, stay on the bus and forget about us.

Respectfully,
W.R. Sigurdson
Director of Civic Events

sealed

THE OLD MAN had a sign he was very proud of. This thing sat outside on a pole, overlooking a cluttered yard full of oil drums, rusting barrels and mud puddles that mirrored the blue Northeastern sky. The sign showed a cartoon box with boxing gloves clutching at its bulging sides. 'I coulda been a container!' it announced disconsolately, referencing a once-famous film now surely lost on most of the passing traffic.

Caudell, driving a large early-model car, pulled in and parked directly at the base of the sign. He climbed out and stood there for a moment, smoking and looking around at the reduced condition of the work yard, He was pale and willowy, his black hair plastered to a small skull. After a moment, he stubbed out his cigarette and went inside to the office, throwing open the door perhaps a bit too vigorously.

The Old Man was at a desk behind the counter. On Caudell's entrance he tilted his head without looking

directly at the younger man. In each hand he held a miniature piece of plastic, extended at arm's length as if about
to connect them like touch wires. The office was absent
of any indoor light and Caudell realised instantly the Old
Man was blind.

'Yessir, what can I do for you?' the Old Man called.
Even from halfway across the room he gave off an intense
tobacco smell.

'I need something canned,' said Caudell.

The Old Man set the bits of plastic down on the desk,
carefully memorising their positions.

'You the fella called earlier? With the maple syrup?'

'No, not maple syrup. I did call, though. No one
answered.'

'I don't answer the phone if I'm here by myself,' said
the Old Man. 'I'll just let it ring. For all I know people
think I'm lying here dead on the floor. Eventually that'll
bring 'em around anyway.'

'Well . . . I saw your name in the paper.'

'Not me. No, sir.'

'Not *your* name. I meant here . . . this company.'

'I ain't even in the phone book,' said the Old Man.
'Pay five dollars extra just for that benefit.'

'That's crazy, isn't it?' said Caudell, aware of the frictionless nature of this banter. He had not talked to another
human being in three days.

'What?'

'That we have to pay *not* to be in the phone book.'

'Some folks just want to be left alone, I suppose,' said
the Old Man. 'Do me a favour, will ya?' He indicated the
floor around his chair. 'See maybe you can find a pair of
tweezers lyin' around here somewhere.'

'Over there?'

'Yeah, just come around the counter. Don't mind the dog.'

170

Caudell stepped around a weary, listless bloodhound who acknowledged his existence by opening one red marbled eye and promptly shutting it again. Caudell found the tweezers on the floor a few feet from the Old Man's chair. He took the Old Man's hand and placed the instrument in his palm. The Old Man's coarse, yellowed fingertips pushed into Caudell's wrist and for a moment he felt as if he were being read. He stood there deferentially, not quite sure what to do with himself, letting the Old Man probe his arm. This felt like a journey to Caudell, though he couldn't say why. He looked down at the desk and saw that the Old Man was building a tiny model ship.

'That's the *Cutty Sark*,' he said.

'Indeed it is,' said the Old Man, finally pulling his hand away.

'I recognise the rigging. Quite a boat, the *Cutty Sark*.'

'I couldn't claim to know much about that. It's canning 'em interests me.'

'You put them in cans?'

'Yessir, I do.'

'Why?'

'It gets slow around here this time of year.'

'Most people build ships in bottles.'

'Yessir, I believe they do.'

'Did you not consider that? So they can be admired?'

'Some people admire a good can.'

'How long have you had this hobby?'

'Well, let's see. It'd be going on thirty-five years or so. When I started, cans was all tin. All my earliest models are tin cans. I reckon they could be worth something.' The Old Man pointed to a shelf above his head, where row after row of shiny ribbed cans sat stacked atop each other.

'Take that big one down,' he instructed.

Caudell pulled down a can the size of something you might see in a restaurant or hospital kitchen.

'That's the *Bonhomme Richard*,' said the Old Man. 'Go ahead, give it a shake.'

Caudell shook the can and it rattled like a collection of loose bones. Whatever ship was in there was clearly dismantled by now.

'Well, it certainly feels seaworthy. But how do I know it's the *Bonhomme Richard* if I can't see it?'

'Because I just told you it was.'

'How long did it take you to build it?'

'Well I slap the ships together in no time. It's canning 'em that's the painstaking part. That one took me a day and a half. It's hand-welded. Those little ribbed deals around the rim are called beads. Every one of them beads has to be perfect.'

'You seem proud of your craft.'

'Yessir, I know my business. I've been at this canning works since 1956. Up until 1998 I was a bottom seamer. Then my eyes went on me.'

'Are you completely blind?'

'I don't need to see to know we've never met before. You from around here?'

'No,' replied Caudell. 'Boston. I drove down from Boston.'

'That's a ways.'

'I don't mind driving. I like to drive the back roads.'

'Why stop here? This place is ruined.'

'To you maybe. Maybe you've been here your whole life. But I have fresh eyes . . . no offence intended. I like to get the local paper and have a look through. Which is where I saw your ad. It made me laugh. You think of that?'

'What?'

'I coulda been a container.'

'Yeah. That's from *On the Waterfront*.'

'I got it. Anyway, it cracked me up.'

Suddenly the Old Man scuddered his chair around, turning his face straight at Caudell. The blueness of his eyes had an intensity that made Caudell believe, for just an instant, that he could actually see.

'Let me ask you a question,' the Old Man said. 'If no one answered the phone, why'd you come here?'

Caudell wondered if the Old Man's cordiality had been a ruse. He chose to answer the question indirectly.

'I need you to can some ashes for me.'

Something flickered in the Old Man's face. Caudell waited. What he needed right now from this old man was a sense of workmanship that would override further questions.

'I can can anything,' the Old Man finally answered. 'In any kind of container. Tin, zinc, electroplate . . . seal 'em near to human perfect. Run your fingers around that lid. I dare you to find a nub.'

Caudell traced the underlid of the can, feeling for imperfections.

'It looks like very good work.'

'Most people don't appreciate a good can. You find any nubs?'

'No. It's a very smooth seal.'

'Seamless. Yessir.'

'It's rare to find someone who takes pride in their work any more.'

'Well, the best work is work you don't see at all.'

Caudell relished the gratuitous tone of this conversation. It had been a long, long ride and it felt good to talk to someone.

'You're absolutely right there. Few people appreciate that. I just rebuilt a bedroom.'

'You don't say,' said the Old Man absently.

'I do say. My ladyfriend, Trina's her name. It's her house, actually . . . We've been together three years. And the place is falling apart. So I did up the bedroom. I'm an ace at that sort of thing. I can wield those angry tools.'

'*Angry* tools?'

'You know. Ripsaw. Sledgehammer. Crowbar. The ones that do a lot of damage in a real short amount of time. And drywalling . . . I can mud up a wall as tight as your cans there. If you can spot the joins in it, I'll kiss your ass in Macy's window.'

'Ho, ho. Macy's window. That's good.' The Old Man laughed at this in the manner of a host, letting Caudell ramble on.

'I mean, this bedroom was pristine. New floor, new wiring, new walls, the whole shebang. Like a dream bedroom. You know?'

'All right.'

'That night, me and Trina drag the bed back in. There's this invigorating waft of new paint and plaster. And we're lying in bed together and I'm looking around . . . You ever have that feeling pass through you where for a second, just a fleeting second, you think, "All right, all right, in this moment everything is *perfect*"?'

'Ahaa . . .'

'Well that's the feeling I have. My spine feels like a picket fence. I'm exhausted but I'm supremely . . . What's the word?'

'Complete,' said the Old Man. 'The sense of *completion*.'

'There's that, but there's something else. *Reparation*. Like, I've paid Trina back. Because she's more or less talked me out of a few scrapes over the years. I've had a rough go of things and she's put up with my bullshit.

174

She sometimes tries to make me out worse than I am, but it's probably for my own good, y'know?'

'Don't tell me. You started thinking of that room as *yours* now.'

'I suppose I did. That's very perceptive.'

'You made a mistake there.'

'Did I? I put in the work. How am I supposed to not help feeling like—'

The Old Man interrupted. 'You only own the creation.'

This illumination startled Caudell. He stopped for a moment and studied the Old Man, whose opalescent eyes seemed now to be reading his mind. He was aware of pouring himself out in this dim, dusty room to someone who might be a sage or possibly demented, but he was thankful for being heard and for telling the truth.

'It was like a new beginning . . .' Caudell said, 'covering up the troubles in those walls, *her* troubles mostly. Her ex-husband tried to put her eye out once in that very room.'

'Lord . . .'

'But that's a story for another day. Anyway . . . we fall asleep. Middle of the night, boom, she's bolt upright.'

'Uh oh.'

'I say, *What?* She says, *That . . . that noise.* I don't hear anything. She says, *Listen.* Then I hear it. A kind of *scritch, scritch. thump, thump* inside the wall . . . my new wall. Now I'm wide awake, trying to fit the sound to some-thing known, dodgy plumbing maybe. But this sounds *alive.* Trina jumps out of bed. She's wide-eyed . . . she's cradling her jaw with her hands like some chick in a horror movie, staring behind the headboard. Then I realise what it is: a goddamned rabbit.'

'Rabbit?'

'Trina's got this four-year-old daughter, Ruby. I'd won

the kid a rabbit at one of them gyppo carnies, and now it appears the stupid thing has managed to entomb itself in my wall. Trina's shitting a brick, screaming, *Oh my God* over and over, which is her ubiquitous response to anything untoward. *Oh my God.* That's just hackneyed coloration if you ask me.

'I'm missing something here,' the Old Man said, confused.

'Doesn't matter. Anyway, she screams, *How did this happen?* I tell her I'm not sure, that I vaguely remember the thing darting in and out of the room while I was putting up wallboard, that it must've got between the support studs right before I sealed it up. Well now Trina starts going nuts, dancing tight circles in the middle of the bedroom, practically ripping the skin off her thighs. *GET THAT POOR ANIMAL OUT NOW!* she yells and now I'm worried she's gonna wake up Ruby, who doesn't need to come in here and discover her goddamned bunny is inside the wall. I climb out of bed to calm Trina down and she grabs the bedstead and heaves the whole bed away from the wall, ripping this raw violent crease into my oak floor, my brand-new oak floor. *Don't suffocate*, she tells the fucking rabbit. *Please don't suffocate. I couldn't ever stand myself.* She's practically caressing the wall. She turns and looks at me . . . looks at me like I'm supposed to do something. But this is the goddamn animal's screw-up, not mine. *Calm down, it's not gonna suffocate,* I say. *It'll find its way up through the heating ducts.* I say this because I want to go back to sleep. I know there are no ducts between those joists. I know the stupid fucking rabbit is wedged between two-by-fours and it's probably shredding itself on dry-wall screws. But I'm not about to point that out to Trina. *Address the problem now*, she says. *I am addressing the problem*, I say. I say, *Here's the thing you need to understand: I've just finished rebuilding this bedroom. And I'll be goddamned if I'm going to tear it all out to rescue some goddamned liquorice-shitting bedroom slipper.* You know what she says?'

'What?

'Well if you did such a mighty job, you can do it again. Oh no, I say, I'm done working on this room. I hold up this finger. You can't see it but it's septic from a bandsaw blade. I say, *Sorry, babe, but that rabbit is just insulation now.* She grabs a pillow and heads to the living room to sleep on the couch. I follow her. She's screaming, *I don't believe you! You're just going to let it starve to death in the bedroom wall!* I say, *You wouldn't be so worked up if it was a rat in there. You only feel sorry for things that have eyebrows. TURN AROUND AND LOOK AT ME! I rebuilt that room from the foundation up. I broke my back while you thumbed through your catalogues and changed your mind about a million goddamn times a day. THAT IS OUR DREAM FUCKING BEDROOM. Now can we please go back in there and fucking dream?* She's giving me this World Wildlife Fund look, calling me an asshole. She says, *I've seriously misjudged you, you fucking asshole!* She pushes past me and storms downstairs to the cellar. And I stand there shaking. A long time ago I promised myself I wasn't going to ever let anyone call me an asshole again. Then I look over and see Ruby crouching in her bedroom doorway. She's scared, sobbing . . . she's clutching this plush toy, this Chicken Little thing. I pick her up and take her back into her bedroom and sit with her on the edge of the bed. I'm trying to calm her. I don't know what to say to her. This is her house too. I just say the simplest things: the words that you would say about a house. *Stone. Wood. Water. Food. Sacrifice.* You see, mister, we are all desperate. And in desperation the simplest words have great calmative powers. Trina comes back upstairs and I see she has my claw hammer, and she goes into our bedroom and defiles my wall, just ripping into it. Every blow makes Ruby and me shudder. And we sit, just the two of us, listening . . . waiting . . . until finally we hear the hammer drop to the floor. I get Ruby snug under her covers, tell her to stay right there. I go into the bedroom. There's dust everywhere. Trina's by the wall and behind her is this hole big enough to walk through. She's cradling the rabbit and goddamn if it isn't dead. All that hammering must've just caused its heart to explode. Trina's laughing, sobbing, hysterical in a hateful kind of way. *I feel sorry for you*, she says to me. *You might be something but you're not a finisher. You're never going to finish anything in your life.* I just stand there for a moment and look around at the room, our perfect room, our perfect room she's just gone and destroyed. Over a fucking rabbit.'

Caudell could no longer tell if he was talking or just thinking all this. The Old Man merely stared off, offering him nothing, no assurance, no understanding, no absolution. Caudell felt as if he were in a dream state, a disquieting dream that suggested he wasn't here at all, that he would awaken somewhere else, that this Old Man might be the last recognisable person he would ever see. He was aware he was sweating now, and wiped his brow with the sleeve of his shirt.

'So you cremated it?' said the Old Man.

'Sorry?'

178

'The rabbit. You want me to seal the rabbit's ashes? For the little girl?'

'Oh. No,' Caudell answered. 'I threw the rabbit in the dump. I, uh . . . I need a fifty-gallon drum.'

best western

RYVITA GRAVES, SEVENTEEN and ready to drop any minute now, didn't know who the baby's father was: didn't know if he was black, white, in-state, out-of-state or Comanche. She might as well have had that motel's sign-in sheet tattooed on her back.

At least that was what her mother said. But Ry wasn't all that worked up about it. She'd seen enough TV to know that situations like this generally ended up okay, and usually in a timely, tidy manner.

'Ry,' Del said.

'What, Mama?'

'Ry, listen to me . . .'

'I'm listening, Mama . . .'

Ry was only half listening. She was sprawled on the wagon-wheel couch trying to watch Springer.

'About the baby . . .'

'What about the baby?'

'If anyone asks who the baby's daddy is . . .'

'Mama. You know I don't know who the baby's daddy is.'

'I know. But if anyone asks . . . I want you to say you don't know, you were raped.'

'I wasn't raped,' she said irritatedly.

'I know, honey, but I think it would be a better explanation.'

'Explanation of what?'

'Can you just look at me for a second? If you were to explain that that baby came about because of a no situation rather than a . . . yes, yes, yes situation . . . it wouldn't be . . . well, as embarrassing.'

'I'm not embarrassed. I'm pregnant.'

'I know, honey, but . . .'

Ry turned on her mother.

'This isn't about me,' she said. 'This is about you. You're ashamed of me!'

'I didn't say ashamed, I said embarrassed.'

'You should be ashamed!' she shrieked. 'You wanna know what people think of you?'

'I don't care what people think of me . . .'

'The hell you don't. They think you're a dyke, Mama . . .' The phone on the lobby desk rang and Del went to get it. Ry was up off the couch, waddling along behind her.

'. . . they think you're a big bull dyke, Mama. They think you're something that fell off Mount Rushmore.'

Del picked up the receiver, cupped her hand over it and screamed at Ry:

'This is about the baby, Ryvita! *Tell them you were raped!*' Then she calmly greeted the caller.

'It's A Del Vista Day. Family-owned and operated. How can I help you?'

*　*　*

182

Ed Kehoe: People ask me, 'Ed, how did you end up becoming an assessor for the Highway Department?' You know what I say? I say, 'Why do you say "end up"?' As if I made a wrong turn somewhere, as if I'm being asked to offer up excuses. I'm fully aware there's no glamour to what I do. But there is satisfaction. Building a road is a project. It has a gradual, cumulative sense of reward. You always gotta look at the big picture. And the big picture is the road.

When I'm assigned a project, I consider each particular property I buy up to be an impediment. Sometimes I have to move people on. I'm not thrilled about that, but here's what you gotta understand: The Highway is Going Through. And the Highway is gonna take the path of least possible resistance. People get all righteous . . . 'We've been here for years.' Well, you gotta remember the road was here first. You built your place here for convenience, fuckface. You've been sucking off the federal tit for gratis and you ought to be a bit more grateful for that. Don't ask me for sympathy, 'cause this ain't a democracy, it's the US Government.

I buy up houses and I buy up businesses. Homeowners aren't usually a problem. No one wants to live near traffic. But businesses . . . they'll give me every sob story in the book. I can waltz into a place, take one look around and see it's dyin' on the vine. Still, they'll cook the books, trot out all kinds of trumped-up profit statements, tell me they're an ongoing concern the public can't live without, a regular hotcake factory. I gotta explain, 'Hey, your business is your business. I don't give a shit. I'm just here for the dirt. I'm here to remove you from the dirt you're sitting on.'

Del Graves was on the phone when Ed Kehoe came in. He stood there in the middle of the lobby, politely waiting for her to finish up. There was a pregnant girl on the couch watching TV. Ed pulled a small disposable camera from his inside jacket pocket and snapped her. Then he snapped the wagon-wheel chandelier, the dilapidated buffalo head mounted above the desk and the Navajo-design carpet, which was threadbare and tattered at the edges.

Document everything.

'Hi,' Del said, hanging up. 'You want a room?'

'I want *all* your rooms,' Ed replied.

'I'm sorry. Run that by me again?'

Ed went over to the desk and delicately deposited a business card, then stepped back, as if it might be a fire-cracker about to go off.

'Ed Kehoe,' he said. 'Department of Transportation. *US* Department of Transportation.'

Del went, 'Oh!' in a slightly startled kind of way and then, for lack of a better word, fairly *bustled.*

'Ryvita, honey,' she said to her daughter, 'why don't you go out to the kitchen, get us some coffee and crackers and Kraft cheese?' The idea was to shuffle her walrus-sized, astoundingly pregnant daughter out of this picture.

'Get 'em yourself, Mama,' Ry replied.

Del apologised. 'Poor girl, she's had some trouble . . .'

'I wasn't raped,' Ry said matter-of-factly.

Del went off for snacks, disappearing through a door behind the desk. Ed walked over to the couch and stood beside Ry. They both watched the TV: Springer was about to reveal the results of a paternity test. The camera cut to a young man shifting insouciantly backstage. The kid had lank brown hair that flopped across one eye, and looked like he was awaiting approval on a car loan application.

Ed said, 'Why do you watch this?'

Ry looked at him strangely. 'Because it's hilarious. It's families working through their problems.'

'I don't watch TV.'

'Some say it's staged but I don't believe it. You can't act that real. I mean look at her. Look at that hair.'

The camera had cut back to a pregnant girl seated on Jerry's stage. The girl wore a T-shirt that read 'Bite Me'. She was cute in a trailer-trash kind of way and you could tell she'd put a lot of thought into choosing that shirt for her national TV debut.

'She don't look much different than you.'

'You shitting me? She's fat. If I end up fat after this baby, I'm going to get one of those staples put in my stomach.'

'You're not fat. You're a fountain of youth.'

'I don't know how anyone couldn't watch TV.'

'Why?'

'Because TV is like pure love. It doesn't judge. If you're really good you get your own show. And if you're really bad . . .' she pumped her fist in the air, '*Jer-ree* . . . you get your own show. If you're on TV it's because TV loves you.'

Del came back in the lobby with a tray of cheese crackers.

'So you two live here?' Ed said.

'We do,' said Del. 'Got a little apartment in the back. We're the only family-owned place on this whole . . .'

Ed told her that would affect the settlement.

'Settlement?'

'Certainly. If this is a residence as well as a business, I'll take that into account. I realise you'll need a new place to live.'

'Hold it,' said Del. 'You got me a little turned around here. I thought we were talking about an easement.'

'Shot who in the where?'

'Way I understand it, from what the DoT letters have said . . . I'm . . . we're . . . entitled to an easement on to the property. From the new road?'

''Scuse me,' Ed said and pulled out a small spiral-bound notebook. 'I just need to corroborate a misunder-standing, make this as plain as I can for you, Del.' Then, in a stentorian tone – whatever that means – he read her the riot act: *This motel and surrounding environs are subject to* force majeure *proceedings, to wit, purchase and removal of said property for the purpose of expanding the adjacent highway to accommodate six lanes of alternate-flow traffic, the construction of which is to begin immediately.*

Del said, 'Speak English.'

'Pack your shit and get out.'

'Whoa . . .'

'I'm sorry. That was a bit abrupt. Not one of my best traits.'

'See if I got this right. You're tellin' us to leave?'

'Your generous government is prepared to pay ten thou-sand dollars per acre. Everything else is gravy. If this decrepit lobby is anything to go by . . .'

'Decrepit?'

'. . . your gravy boat sank a long time ago.'

'This is an accredited motel.'

'Can I finish? You'll be reimbursed for all future reser-vations, assuming they're guaranteed.'

'Mr Kehoe . . .'

'Call me Ed.'

'Ed. You can't just march right in here . . .'

'This is where you do your little righteous indigna-tion dance? Go on. I'll be right over here.' Ed scarfed a cracker from the tray, then began wandering around the lobby taking snapshots. From the couch, Ryvita said, 'I saw all about this on a TV show. It's called immaculate domain . . .'

'Eminent domain,' Ed corrected her, rolling his eyes.

'That's it. There was this farmer who refused to leave, and the bulldozers just ploughed right through.'

'Snakebelly.'

'*Snakebelly?*'

'They snakebellied the fella. Built the highway on either side of him. No way in, no way out. He lasted about a year.'

'You wouldn't do that to us would you?'

'My worst trait . . .' Ed said, 'let's just go right to my very worst trait . . . the mistaken belief that I actually enjoy this part of my work.'

'Whose mistaken belief?'

'Because I don't. But there's an army of road workers over the horizon and my job is to remove any impediment to their progress.'

'We aren't impediments,' said Ry. 'We're people.'

'You want me to assess you as a person? Okay. You're barefoot, pregnant and dumb as a stick. But I can't assign a value to that.' Ed turned to Del. 'I can, however, tell you that it's a health violation to employ a woman in the final trimester of her pregnancy. I report that, it's gonna cost you a thousand dollars. See how this works?'

'This place is worth far more than ten thousand dollars an acre,' Del said defensively.

'Tell it to the marines.'

He removed a large yellow envelope from his jacket pocket and slapped it on top of the desk. Then he pulled himself up and perched, rubbing the circulation back into his leg.

'Two guesses what's in there and your first one's wrong. It's a writ from the State of Montana to vacate or else.'

'Or else what?'

'There is no or else what.'

'How can . . . We get people from all over the world staying here . . .'

Ryvita chimed in. 'We had a family from Australia last week.'

'Well have 'em write me a letter. I collect stamps.'

'Peter Fonda stayed here once,' Ry said. 'Peter Fonda? *Easy Rider*?'

Ed thought for a minute.

'Nope. Nothing's comin' to mind.'

'People come back here every year . . .' Del said. There was a fissure in her voice now. 'Ask for the same room . . .'

'Del . . .'

'They bring their kids and those kids bring their kids . . .'

'Del! My give-a-shit is broke, okay?'

He lowered himself from the desk and approached her.

'I checked your tax records. You're four years in arrears. Did you know that?'

'I'm just trying to make a go of things. It's difficult. Can you understand that?'

'You are entitled to a resettlement fee.'

Del fixed her face in a bulldog stare. 'I like it here just fine.'

'I can't help you, Del,' Ed said, softening. He actually felt a little sorry for this dilapidated motel with its struggling neon and its mom-and-pop quality, minus the pop.

'Listen,' he explained, 'it might be different if this place had some charm or historical significance. But look at it. No one wants to remember the seventies.' He looked around at the sad Western motif. 'The *eighteen*-seventies. You can't even see it, can you?'

'See what?'

Ed hobbled over to the big picture window that faced out to a highway nobody used any more.

'It's my job to know what the public wants. And the public wants big, bland uniformity. The public wants an exit ramp that leads to a big, bland Best Western and a big, bland all-you-can-eat buffet restaurant across from a big, bland fill 'er-up emporium. The public doesn't have any wistful notions any more of the road *calling its name,* all that Route 66 shit.' He turned from the window to Del. 'You want nostalgia, buy it at the Cracker Barrel.'

Del walked over and shoved the envelope into his chest.

'I'm not signing anything,' she said.

Ed sighed.

'Del. You'll be forcibly removed.'

'You're a callous prick, aren't you?'

'You don't know me from the wallpaper. I'm just a man doing a job. Same as you.' He pushed the envelope back at her, then crossed the lobby and paused at the door.

'I'm gonna be here first thing tomorrow morning, Miss Del, to start surveying. In the meantime, I was you I'd do some landscaping, put in some Rainbird sprinklers. Ups the value.'

Ry had been watching this unfold like some kind of TV drama.

'Why?' she said. 'You're just gonna tear it all up.'

Ed gave her a wink.

'Government works in mysterious ways, miss.'

I make a good wage, decent benefits, full medical. Coupla years back, a 'dozer bucket shattered my pelvis. OSHA sent me into the hospital for a new hip. To be honest, I woulda preferred titanium, but the government ... you can't negotiate with a shark. In the operating room, goin' under, I watched 'em pull it out of a box: bone stem and socket. It said 'Manufactured in Taiwan' on the side: cheap plastic, like a doggy squeak toy, vinyl or something. Six months later I'm barbecuing elk steaks in the back yard and all of a sudden I start listing to one side. Goddamn if I didn't melt the cheap sonofabitch leanin' over the coals. They replaced it, but the doc told me some of the plastic had migrated through my prostate wall and into my fellas. You understand? I'm shootin' plastic bullets. The wife and I had been tryin' for a baby. She's forty-one now, thinking the last boat's left the dock, making over-tures about adopting, which is a right royal bureaucratic clusterfuck. Finding someone who wants to give up a white kid these days that isn't already addicted to crystal meth or been dropped in a puddle of Aids is tantamount to imfuckingpossible. Frankly, I don't know what to do about it. Frankly, I think the whole marriage is on the fritz. Frankly, I never was much of a people person.

Later that afternoon:

'What is it that I'm not understanding, Mama?'

'My position. Our position.'

'Our position is . . .'

'We used to get families here. Station wagons full of 'em. Sounds of laughter, hopefulness. Daytimes were loud and nighttimes were quiet. Now . . . it's the other way around. Doors slamming, cars driving off, rustbuckets with cowshit hanging off the mudflaps. People screamin' blue murder. Shootin' up TV sets.'

Ry laughed.

'You think it's funny?'

'It *is* funny.'

'Look, you want to sit here with your feet up and let the government rob us? Or do you want to do something about it?'

'Well what exactly?'

'We fill up the res book.'

'With what?'

'With names.'

'What names?'

'From these old receipts.'

Del held up a bundle of old receipts she kept in a cardboard box.

'And the credit card numbers. Some in your handwriting, some in mine, so it looks authentic.'

'Mama, there's two cars in the parking lot . . .'

'Well guess what . . . suddenly it's going to be a monster summer. Like in the old days. Remember how it felt to hang up that No Vacancy sign? Fill it up, Ryvita, charge the full whack . . . that's fifty, sixty thousand dollars' worth of business they gotta reimburse us for. You know a better way?'

'This isn't right, Mama.'

'What's right any more? I've got a family to provide for. Some people have no respect for that. And that Ed fella has terrible manners. '

She pushed the reservation book toward Ry.

'Now, honey . . . write.'

Del Graves: I suppose I'm motelled out these days. But oh God, what a time I had watching people come through here, taking in the West for the first time. It made me jealous, like I'd been cheated of that particular elation. Sometimes I look back at my life and it's like I read it. The way I just slipped from one life into another seems like someone else's story. We make mistakes. We move on. Your life's your own business.

When I was young, the only men around here were railroaders and cowboys. The railroaders always seemed to look through me. I met this cowboy and he looked right at me. His name was Early Graves. He came into town to buy bulls and left with me, said he had an eye for perfection: that was our joke. He took me up to a ranch, and the minute I saw it I told him it was the prettiest thing I'd ever seen. I knew that was what he wanted to hear. Truth is, it scared me to death. You look at that place, the beauty and the brutality of it, and you realise soon enough it doesn't care if you're happy or sad, if you live or if you die. It just doesn't care. The more frightened I got, the more he pushed me away. What was I supposed to do? He claims I never came to terms with the satisfaction of it, but the truth is, I just wanted a more domestic life is all. When Ry was born, he wasn't even there. He'd gone to Billings with some cattle, and when he got back and saw I'd had a little girl, he didn't even try to hide his disappointment. I guess he just thought it was going to be a boy, someone to follow him around like one of his calves and learn the ranch. He plopped Ryvita down in front of the TV set and pretty much forgot about her.

I put up with it for a year. Then one day I took Ryvita and left, just like that. Went back to Billings and I took up with a railroader. When the railyards went bust we bought this motel, ran it together. The yards picked up again and that railroader was gone in a flash. So I've seen both sides of the coin. Leaving and being left. And I'll tell you, it's better to stay. Things can possibly be fixed by staying. I know that now.

* * *

He showed up here once, Early. Strode right in through those doors and said, 'Hello, Del.' We talked for a while, and do you know, he never once asked about Ry? Didn't say how is she or kiss my ass. And he'd gone a little soft. He'd had a heart scare and driven himself in to see the doctor. It had all checked out okay, but I think, for just a moment, that bastard had gotten reflective. Because as he was leaving, he stopped in the middle of the lobby and took off his hat and said:

'I never figured I deserved you, Del.'

I said: 'What?'

He said: 'The way you looked. Like when you see a reflection in water, shimmering, and you know the slightest misstep, the slightest ripple dissolves it. So you don't do anything.' Imagine that black-hearted bastard saying something like that.

I said: 'You're about fifteen years too late with that explanation, Early. But it's okay now.'

He said: 'I got old, Del.'

I said it again: 'It's okay, Early.'

He said: 'Nah. I got old. You got ugly. I guess we're even.'

Ed stood in the forecourt of the Ridgecrest Trailer Park, which was basically nothing more than a breeding ground to ensure both NASCAR and the state penitentiary a future supply of enthusiasts, and stared across the road into the lobby of the Del Vista. He could see Ry at the desk, scribing diligently into a red book, like a child struggling with homework. There was no traffic out here, just the sound of a dog drinking from the trailer park swimming pool, and far in the distance, the drone of the methane plant. He stared up at the moon, which was practically full, and tried to make out a face. There *was* one all right, but it was his wife's: sullen and vindictive and mouthing big silvery globules of profanity that essentially imputed her current state of childlessness squarely in his lap. He, in turn, blamed this generally on the Montana Department of Transportation, and specifically on a bulldozer operator who had been too engrossed in a *Modern Hunter* article on proper field dressing of the elk to notice Ed walking in front of his bucket.

Now he was just going to have to let the worst of his instincts take over.

'Hello there.'

'Hi.'

'I brought you these.' He handed her a spray of flowers. Protruding from the middle was a large white wooden cross.

'Sorry about the barefoot, dumb and pregnant thing. I'm not always up on my people skills.'

'Uhhhh . . . thanks,' Ry answered, eyeing the flowers dubiously. 'Did you get these from the side of the road?'

'Yeah,' he said. 'I've been driving up and down the highway pulling them up,' then added, 'Part of my job.' In Montana, roadside flowers were used to mark the site of a traffic fatality.

'That's kinda creepy.'

'Not at all. It's beautiful out there at night. Not much traffic.'

'There never is.'

Ed went over to the window and stared out.

'Just the full moon shining on the asphalt. Like a motionless river. Amazing what you can see under a full moon.'

'I guess so.'

'I can stand out there and see you plain as day.'

194

'You were watchin' me?'

'Watched you beavering away at that reservation book.'

He went over to Ry and draped himself across the desk.

'So. How's business?'

'We're looking real good for the summer. That's . . . our busy season.'

'You must think I just fell into the daisy patch,' he said, and instantly his disposable camera was out, snapping a picture of the receipts, the res book, Ry's flagrante delicto endeavour.

She panicked.

'I'm just doin' what Del told me to do,' she said.

'Of course you are,' Ed answered, smiling. The smile was meant to absolve her. In fact it looked perfectly fatuous.

'Mr Kehoe?' she said.

'Ed. Call me Ed. I beg you.'

'If there's not much traffic out there, how come you're widenin' the road?'

'Well now, Ryvita, that's a good question. Why don't we sit down?'

'Sure. If you wanna.'

Ed took her arm and walked her over to the couch. With bovine grace, he eased her on to the cushions, and came back up slightly bent at the waist, indicating a small degree of spinal damage. Then he sat down, practically *on top* of her.

'Think of a road as a living thing,' he began, straining for an allegory. 'A natural extension of humanity.'

'Okay.'

'And . . . much like yourself . . .' he plopped an awkward hand on to her bump, 'it has to expand to accommodate growth.'

'But there's—'

'Yes. I know. There's not much traffic. Sometimes a road has to expand because humans are irresponsible.'

He took the flowers from her and set them on the coffee table.

'These white crosses, Ryvita. What do they represent?'

'Accidents.'

'They represent people, Ryvita. Careless people. Reckless people. People who've made a mistake. Who weren't prepared for the curves the road threw at them.'

'Oh. Right.'

'What about you, Ryvita?' He drummed his fingers across her belly. 'Are you prepared for all the curves ahead?'

'What?'

'Would you call yourself a responsible driver?'

'Yeah . . .'

'Are you sure about that? Haven't you been a little careless?'

'I don't know. Maybe a little.'

'Who's the father, Ryvita?'

'I'm not sure. I got it narrowed down to a list of about six.' She shifted uneasily. 'Ed?'

'Yes?'

'You're makin' me a little uncomfortable. You mind if I turn on the TV?'

'Go ahead,' he said,

'You can sit here as long as you like. But I don't want to talk about my baby any more.'

'Okay.'

She stared vacantly into the TV. Ed rose and walked around behind the couch, frustrated. Things had been ripening to a degree and then she'd gone for the remote.

Suddenly she said:

'It's gonna be fine. A baby don't take up a whole lotta room.'

'Yes it does, Ryvita. It takes up your whole life.'

'I seen this programme about Eskimo babies. All the women—'

He leaned over the back of the couch and grabbed her shoulders.

'Do you believe in love at first sight?'

'What!'

'Love at first sight. Do you believe such a thing can happen between two people?' He was aiming, here, for poignancy.

'Like *Sleepless in Seattle*?'

'Sure. Like *Sleepless in Seattle*.'

'You liked that movie?'

'I did.' He had no idea what movie she was talking about.

'Yeah, me too.'

'If you can imagine love at first sight . . . can you imagine a love of family at first sight?'

'What are you gettin' at, Ed?'

He wheeled around the side of the couch and, owing to the rigid mechanics of one artificial hip, somewhat hydraulically lowered himself to one knee.

'I'd like to help look out for your baby.'

'Why?'

That was a question impossible to explain. He had no grasp of incipient fatherhood, just an obligation to placate his wife. For all he knew, he might just possibly plop the thing on the doorstep of his own home, ring the bell and run for the hills. All he could think to say was:

'I'm drawn to you.'

'I think Del might have somethin' to say about that.'

'You're a grown woman, Ryvita. You tell me . . . you think we could be friends? A baby needs a father. A father figure.'

'Yeah. We could be friends.'

'Can I take you out sometime?'

'Where?'

'Anywhere you want to go. You like steaks? I know a great steakhouse.'

'I don't know. I look like a walrus. People'd just stare at me all night long.'

Ed pushed himself up and went to the window.

'We could just drive up on the ridge and park and watch the road in the moonlight,' he said.

'Park?' Aside from TV, this was Ryvita's other major pastime.

'Watch the headlights snake up the highway. Have one last look before they tear it all up.'

'Well, I'm off tomorrow. I could go out tomorrow night.'

'That would be delightful.'

'After *Dancing with the Stars*? It's over by eight.'

'All right. Eight o'clock it is.'

'You aren't gonna stand me up, are ya?'

'No. Of course not. I'll be here.'

'All right.'

'I just gotta clear it with my wife.'

'You gotta wife?'

'Yeah,' he said painfully. 'I got a wife.'

He was rapidly approaching the point of no return. A man frightened of his own marriage can choose to save it or ruin it. He knew that. But there was nothing to do now but go for it and assess the damage later.

'Come to the window,' he said. 'I want to show you something.'

He helped her off the couch and over to the window, her eyes following the TV screen as if she were drifting away from a life raft.

'See that trailer park? The sodium lights?'

'Yeah.'

'See the empty lot? To the right of the cottonwood.'

'Okay.'

'If you wanted that spot, Ryvita . . . your own little spot . . . I could get that for you.'

'I don't have a trailer.'

'I'm gonna buy you a trailer.'

'A new one?'

'Stickers still on the windows. Set you up real nice. And you know what else?'

'What else?'

'A forty-two-inch genuine plasma high-definition TV. With satellite. What would you say to that?'

'I'd say, *Hello, forty-two-inch genuine plasma high-definition TV. With satellite.*'

'In fact, I reckon a TV that big, you'd need a double wide to hold it.'

'Oh my God. I feel like I'm on *Let's Make a Deal.*'

'Well we are making a deal, aren't we?'

'I'll hafta think about this,' she said and shuffled back to the couch. Ed trailed right behind her.

'You absolutely should think about it. Think what's best for you and what's best for the baby.'

'The baby.'

'In the long term.'

'Could I come visit it any time I want?'

'Absolutely. Any time, day or night.'

'You don't think your wife will get . . . you know . . .'

'Protective?'

'Yeah. What if she just runs me off? Or takes out one of them injunctions.'

'She won't do that, Ryvita. She'll be indebted to you for life.' He sat down beside her.

Ryvita slid her hands under her legs and looked at the TV as if it might hold the answer to whatever she decided next. There was not even the beginning of a thought on her face. Outside the wind kicked up, slapping a flag against a metal post. Ed marvelled at the absolute hollowness of this girl, this product of America. It wasn't until the TV went to a commercial that she piped up again.

'I ain't prying or nothin', but . . . how come you two can't . . . you know . . .'

'Conceive? The short version is I had an accident. Now, Ryvita, this is between us, right?'

'Yeah.'

'It's a little complicated . . . the adoption process. There's paperwork, blood tests, case-worker visits. People are going to try and sway you.'

'You mean Del.'

'You're going to have to tell her.'

'She's gonna go perfectly apeshit.'

'You have to stand on it.'

There was a long, awkward pause. Maybe not awkward, but certainly a prelude to underscore the gravity of what he was about to say next.

'Unless you want to consider the option.'

'What's that?'

'The option is Del goes to prison.'

'*Prison?*'

'Ryvita, your mama's tampering with the books, thinking she'll get more money from the government. That's fraud.'

Ry frowned, seeming to give this idea careful consideration. Then she said:

'Prison for how long?'

He raised both palms in a gesture of non-interference.

'Not for me to decide. All I'm gonna do is file the assessment the way I read it. I'm gonna keep her little secret between us. Unless she stands in the way. You gotta be persuasive with her, Ryvita.'

'It's my baby. Not hers. I can do what I want with it.'

That was all he needed to hear.

'I'm your best friend now, Ryvita,' he said. 'Ryvita? Am I your friend?'

He was thinking of his own desires now. As only a small man in a small position of power can, he was aiming for spoils.

'I want you to be.'

He flung his arms around her burgeoning stomach.

'You're a very . . . firm . . . woman.'

'I'm not firm. I'm big.'

'Big but delectable. Like a pumpkin.'

'Well . . . maybe you ought to go.'

'Why?'

'This is starting to feel a little personal.'

'Why? Because I'm talking about you and not your baby? Don't you like the attention?'

She giggled.

'You should go . . .'

'You shy? Ryvita, that it? You shy?' He tickled her belly. 'You shy?'

'No. I'm not shy.'

'I know you're not.' His hands moved to her wrists. 'You're firm.'

'Why are you grabbing my wrist?'

'Because I think you want me to. Because you were made to be squeezed. Like a pumpkin.'

'Owww. Mr Kehoe . . .'

'You like this. Just a little bit, don't you?'

'No.'

'Just a little bit.'

'Maybe . . .'

'You do, don't you? You're a pumpkin, aren't you? You Daddy's little pumpkin?'

'You're pressing too close to me. You're crushing my . . .'

'Tell me you're Daddy's little pumpkin.'

'Pumpkin.'

'You're gonna talk to your mama, aren't you?'

'I already said I would.'

'And you're going to be very persuasive, aren't you?'

'I already said . . . I'm getting very hot.'

'I know you are. You're hot in here, aren't you?' He tapped her belly.

'I meant . . . it's hot.'

'You swallow a candle?'

'What?'

'You must've swallowed a candle.' He swept around and buried his head in her belly. 'Ryvita, after the baby . . .'

'Yeah?'

'You keep that candle burning for me. Any time I want.'

'Okay.'

'I'm looking at the big picture.'

'The big picture.'

'Think of the big picture.'

He pulled out his camera, held it at a distance and said: 'Smile.'

Ryvita watches TV: one of those collapsed-time dramas, set in a Boston hospital.

'I want to listen to your belly,' a nurse says, placing a stethoscope to a young girl's stomach. The girl has a tattoo of a Chinese dragon running up her leg.

She listens for a moment and says: 'It's fine. Thumping like a March hare.'

*The girl with the dragon asks if she can listen. The
nurse lets her, and after a moment the girl pulls the stethoscope from her ears, looks at the floor and says, 'This
baby is going to bring me good luck.'*

'I'm sure it will,' says the nurse.

The girl says: 'Does it make you feel hopeful?'

'What?'

*'Hearing something come into the world, when you're
around so many about to leave.'*

*'What I think,' says the nurse, 'is hope doesn't make
that kind of distinction.'*

*Ryvita likes the girl's tattoo and wishes she had one
like it. Welded to the reality of TV, she changes her mind.*

'It's that time,' Ed said to Del.

'What time is that, Ed?'

'Time to look at the numbers. I finished the survey.
Six acres and some change. You can consider the main
structure and outbuildings as so much firewood. Ditto the
furnishings. I need to see some real value. I need to see
the reservations book.'

'It's right there.'

'Mama . . .' Ryvita said, weakly. From the couch she
could see what was afoot here but was incapable of
bringing herself to account. The idea always was to ignore
the general horror of life and find something to look
askance at.

'Watch TV, hon.'

Ed opened the red ledger and looked through it,
whistling dispassionately.

'You're a busy woman, Del. June, July, August, tight
as a drum. Peak rates.'

'We do gangbusters in the summer.'

'Is that so?'

'Everyone wants to see the buffalo.'

'Are there still buffalo, Del?'

'Of course there's still buffalo.'

'Then I guess that explains why *I'm* being buffaloed,' he said. ''Cause I've already checked your phone records. Quiet as an ant pissing on cotton. You make these reservations telepathically? You know it's a federal crime to report false earnings to the US Government. You aware of that, Del?'

'Ed,' Ryvita blurted, 'I've changed my mind.'

Ed wheeled on her.

'You can't change your mind. It's too late.'

'What are you two talking about?' Del asked, coming out from behind the desk.

'We made a policy.'

'What!'

'A policy.'

'A *policy*?'

'A good-neighbour policy, Del. Ever heard of the good-neighbour policy?'

'What's he mean, Ryvita?'

'Ed was going to take the baby for me, Mama. He was going to look after it.'

'Oh sweet Christ.'

'I was gonna tell you. I was.'

'Okay, change of plans,' Ed said. 'You know, Ryvita, in the penitentiary they take away your baby.'

'You get the hell outta here!' Del seethed.

'Mama . . .'

'Del? You need to look at me right now like I'm your good angel.'

'Get out!'

'Look at me . . .'

'Mama . . .'

'*Look at me!* You two are going away with nothing!'

'We're not going anywhere,' Del said. If Ed had bothered to ask anyone around these parts, they would have told him that Del was not someone you wanted to mess with and that she kept a baseball bat behind the lobby desk for just these kinds of infringements. When she retrieved it and stalked toward him, he tried to back away, but came up against the side of the couch.

'Okay, this isn't necessary . . .' he protested. An hour earlier he had been at the Optimists Club luncheon, enjoying a smothered pork chop. Now things were going from bad to—

She axed him neatly between the hip and short ribs. He crumpled, then tried to raise himself back up and fix her with a baleful stare. She faltered slightly but did not, you could see, deviate from her present course.

'*You* look at *me*, Ed. You seeing me? 'Cause I'm tired of people looking through me!'

'I see you, Del. All right? You have my attention.'

'You believe in God, Ed?'

'What? I don't . . .'

'I asked Ryvita once if she believed in God. Know what she said? She said, *No, because I've never seen him on TV.*' She cackled. 'Isn't that crazy?'

Ryvita had turned on *The Price Is Right.* A buoyant couple in matching pink T-shirts laced their hands together and waited breathlessly for the pronouncement of the host. All the windows to their future were, in this moment, wide open, and when it turned out to be a lifetime's supply of potato salad, they couldn't have been more thrilled, hugging each other in connubial bliss. Ryvita looked down between her legs and observed something viscous.

'Mama . . .' she said.

'Lock the front door, honey.'

'Mama . . .'

'*Do what I told you!* Well I do, Ed. I believe in God. And I believe God will forgive me for what I'm going to do to you.' She prodded him with the end of the bat.

'Del . . .'

'Shut up! *I'm sick of it, Ed.*'

She cracked the bat down on the wooden arm of the sofa.

'Men!' she screamed. 'Furtive men like you, real shit-kickers . . . they hang around this lobby at night and chat her up . . .' she looked at Ryvita, 'promising you . . . I don't know what they promise . . . to take you away from here? But they never do, do they, honey? *They just take the towels!*'

She dropped the bat on the floor, sat down on the edge of the sofa and raised her eyes toward the ceiling.

You can have it, she thought. *Here are the keys to the motel and all the grimy things in it, the broken-down furniture and stacks of old receipts. That buffalo head hasn't been dusted in ten years. I hope you find it a good home. My soul is shot to shit and I don't know where I'm getting off next. I have brought this on myself.*

'My waters broke,' Ryvita announced, glumly.

Ed Kehoe: Ain't this a sonofabitch. Ain't this a sonof-abitch! This time I am definitely holding out for titanium. Explain to me how God in all his munificence grants these people the miracle of a family, and me, a decent tax-paying individual . . . not to mention a member of the Optimists Club . . . is denied the opportunity to perpet-uate the human race. You ask me, the current crop of kids is just about the biggest bunch of slack-jawed, snot-nosed imbeciles you could imagine. I reckon the pendulum's about to swing. I reckon the next batch will be everything this one ain't.

The thing is, here's the thing. You gotta know when you're whipped. You gotta accept when you're on the losing end. That's me. I'm on the losing end. Last of the Kehoes. End of the road. How can that be?

I build 'em, for chrissakes.

the author, <u>richard travis hall</u>, messes around with an online anagram generator, then attempts to crack the lucrative porn market

H.L. *'RAVI' LARDCH, sitar* extraordinaire, was at his wits' end trying to find a suitable vocalist who could handle the range of his compositions. The Lydian scale of the recordings demanded a singer with a dynamic vocal range, someone who could hit the *rich larval thirds* (and extended ninths) an *H.L. Ravi Lardch sitar* composition demanded. In short what he needed was someone with a *shrill diva catarrh*.

To this end, he had enlisted the services of *Vallari 'Trash' Chard*, a chanteuse of some repute, who sang in a kind of *arch, avid, shrill art*, no doubt, but someone who was more renowned for her sexual appetite, which kept men in an *acrid ravish thrall.*

Unfortunately, *Vallari Trash Chard* was nowhere to be found. It was late and the studio was costing him a fortune.

Ravi looked at his watch then strode over to the recording desk, where his engineer, *Dr Art Chirvis (halal),* was busy trying to retrieve something from inside the mixing console.

'Where the hell is my singer?' he demanded.

'*Chard's arrival halt,*' mumbled Art, who for some odd reason liked to talk like an American Indian, even though he was a devout Muslim.

'What are you doing to the mixing console?' asked Ravi.

'*Trivial, Larch. Shard* of fibreglass fall in to console. Hopefully not a problem.'

'It's Lardch. There's a hard D in my name. How many times do I have to remind you? Have you heard from the record company?'

'*RCA had thrills, Ravi.*'

'That's wonderful news. Hopefully they'll throw some money behind this one.'

'*H.R. Larch ad vital, sir.*'

'L. It's H.L. Lardch. Not H.R. Larch.'

'Yessir.'

Suddenly, *Vallari Trash Chard* slung through the studio doors accompanied by a virile-looking man whom Ravi recognised instantly as the washed-up tenor and all-around ladies' man, *Sir V. 'Carat Hard' Hill.* It was obvious the two had been dining together. Maybe it was the champagne or maybe it was the *caviar's hard thrill,* but Sir V. was in a state of priapic tumescence, his massive organ looking like some kind of *vicar's hard-hat drill*. He was naked from the waist down, wearing only an *archival lard shirt*. Vallari herself seemed to be in the grip of some kind of wanton musth, her face flushed, red as *a lit radish*.

'*Cha, lrrv,*' she said in her broad Yorkshire accent.

'What's he doing here?' barked Ravi. 'This is a closed session.'

'I'll have you know, my good man,' roared Sir Hill, 'I can sing as well as anyone.' This was an idle boast. Everyone knew that his singing days were well behind him, ever since he'd been diagnosed with laryngeal problems, the result no doubt of wearing his silk neckties too tight.

'Nonsense,' laughed Ravi. 'Everyone knows a *cravat rash rid Hill* of his talent years ago!'

'You impugn my dignity!' cried Sir Hill. 'Give me those charts. I'll show you I'm the man for the job.' He barricaded himself in the recording booth and attempted to croon, but could only manage a drunken cacophonous slurry.

'*La la vrrrrid ach, shit!*'

Vallari Trash Chard meanwhile had thrown herself on to an overstuffed armchair, legs splayed, offering her moist tidal pool to all and sundry.

'Who here wants to perform the *chair rash vat drill*?' she slurred.

Everyone hesitated.

'C'mon somebody, eat me,' she demanded.

'*Art, ravish Chard, I'll* handle that idiot Sir Hill,' instructed Ravi, but *Dr Art Chirvis (halal)* was appalled. For him, this entire sordid tableau was deeply offensive to his religious sensibilities.

Eventually, Sir Hill extricated himself from the

recording booth and challenged *Vallari Trash Chard* to a 'fuck grudge match' the winner of whom would receive the recording contract. In no time the two were going at it like animals, a visceral lust borne of competitive rage.

'Latch hard, viral sir,' she moaned.

'Arch hard, rival slit,' he shouted back, pounding her mercilessly.

'Ravish, drill. Ah! Itch!'

'Rah, rah, sir. All is VD.'

And so on.

Things Snowball

'I stopped off at the Peace Gardens – a memorial straddling
the US-Canadian border commemorating "Lasting Peace
Between America and Canada", as if there had ever been a
problem. Show me a garden commemorating Peace Between
America and, say, Iraq and I'll be impressed.
America is like a beauty contestant. It's gorgeous, until it
opens its mouth.'

From the similarities between US gun laws and British
drinking hours, to what cryptic crosswords really tell us
about the British psyche, American in London Rich Hall
casts a keen eye on the lunatic contradictions and weird
marvels of his native and adoptive homelands.

978-0-349-11576-4

Otis Lee Crenshaw

The memoir of Otis Lee Crenshaw, Rich Hall's Perrier
Award-winning alter ego

'My Old Man's name was Jack Daniels Crenshaw. No
surprise what he liked to drink. As a very small child I
remember teething – cryin' out savagely for relief.
Eventually he would appear over my crib and rub Jack
Daniels on his gums until he fell asleep.'

Married six times, all to women named Brenda, Otis Lee
Crenshaw's bourbon-fuelled odyssey takes him from the
high mountains of East Tennessee to the bottom of the
music charts. A man not above faking his own death to sell
more records, this is his not quite true story of romance,
recidivism, country music, and an unshakeable belief in
Marriage at First Sight.

978-0-349-11819-2

Other bestselling titles available by mail:

| ☐ Things Snowball | Rich Hall | £6.99 |
| ☐ Otis Lee Crenshaw | Rich Hall | £7.99 |

The prices shown above are correct at time of going to press. However, the publishers reserve the right to increase prices on covers from those previously advertised, without further notice.

———————————————————— sphere ————————————————————

Please allow for postage and packing: **Free UK delivery.**
Europe; add 25% of retail price; Rest of World; 45% of retail price.

To order any of the above or any other Sphere titles, please call our credit card orderline or fill in this coupon and send/fax it to:

Sphere, P.O. Box 121, Kettering, Northants NN14 4ZQ
Fax: 01832 733076   Tel: 01832 737526
Email: aspenhouse@FSBDial.co.uk

☐ I enclose a UK bank cheque made payable to Sphere for £. . . . .
☐ Please charge £ . . . . . . to my Visa, Delta, Maestro.

Expiry Date ☐☐☐☐   Maestro Issue No. ☐☐

NAME (BLOCK LETTERS please) . . . .

ADDRESS . . . .

. . . .

. . . .

Postcode . . . . Telephone . . . .

Signature . . . .

Please allow 28 days for delivery within the UK. Offer subject to price and availability.